PRAISE FOR
IN DEFENSE OF GUILT

"Through edgy protagonist and defense attorney Lauren Hill, Berkley places us in the midst of a murder trial that could itself be the backbone of an exciting legal thriller—but the metaphysical twist that threatens to change the trial into Hill's own Judgment Day takes *In Defense of Guilt* to the next level."

—CHRISTOPHER LEIBIG
Author of *Almost Mortal* (2016 Indie Book Award)

"*In Defense of Guilt* is a fast-paced legal thriller with a spiritual twist. Benjamin Berkley has crafted a main character who fears no consequences until she goes on trial before the 'ultimate arbiter.' She defends her client accused of murder while wrestling with her own demons of infidelity, greed and lust. Is salvation the light at the end of the tunnel? Well written and highly recommended."

—MELANIE BRAGG
Author of *Crosstown Park,* an Alex Stockton legal thriller

"*In Defense of Guilt* is a modern-day parable that turns a murder trial on its 'ear.' And you'll have to read to the end to see what happens to hard-charging defense attorney Lauren Hill, who confronts God in her courtroom."

—BETSY ASHTON
Author of the Mad Max mystery series, *Unintended Consequences, Uncharted Territory*, and *Unsafe Haven*

"With *In Defense Of Guilt*, Mr. Berkley has written a compellingly unconventional courtroom drama. This unique and fascinating story keeps the reader guessing from beginning to end, while offering an inspirational message that extends far beyond the guilt or innocence of the accused. A truly enjoyable read."

–JOHN J. JESSOP
Author of *Pleasuria*

"When they open Ben Berkley's *In Defense of Guilt*, readers have every reason to expect a page-turner about murder, sex, and the law. What they get is a page-turner of a very different sort. By the time the judge is transformed into God, and smart, sexy attorney Lauren Hill discovers herself accused of the Seven Deadly Sins, there's no going back for Berkley's characters or his readers. Unfortunately, the only person to witness any of this is Lauren herself. Is it fantasy or reality? And does it matter? Instead of a book about murder and sex and the law, expect a book whose themes are forgiveness and love and redemption."

–DEAN ROBERTSON
Author of *Looking for Lydia; Looking for God*

In Defense of Guilt
by Benjamin H. Berkley

ISBN 978-1-63393-652-2

Published by

 köehlerbooks ™

210 60th Street
Virginia Beach, VA 23451
800–435–4811
www.koehlerbooks.com

IN DEFENSE OF
GUILT

BENJAMIN H. BERKLEY

VIRGINIA BEACH
CAPE CHARLES

DEDICATION

To my grandchildren: Dylan, Tess, Raya, Ira, and Simon.
You have been an amazing gift for me, for all you have been,
for all you are, and for all you are yet to be.

CHAPTER ONE

L auren Hill strode toward her place at the defense table, her vigorous, long gait slapping her black heels on the marble floor. Her posture erect and sure, she pointed her nose upward and cast a disgusted look at the prosecution. Her perfect courtroom record afforded her unsurpassed self-assurance. So did her looks.

Although much closer to middle age than she ever cared to admit, Lauren still appeared youthful. With her blonde hair cut in stylish layers, radiant cobalt eyes, flawless creamy complexion, and enviable figure, she turned many heads, and she knew it.

Stepping in front of the leather desk chair, Lauren tucked her pleated skirt under her shapely legs. It was borderline courtroom-inappropriate, but she did not care. Why should she? Her features were God-given and finely honed. She was well-bred, well-manicured, and sophisticated; she exuded a graceful elegance, poise, and charm more befitting a Versace runway than a Los Angeles County courtroom.

With puppy-eyed sappiness, her youthful associate Ryan Thompson leaned over to her ear. "You look awesome."

Seductively crossing her legs, she winked smugly and whispered, "I know."

Her matchless beauty was a clever ruse. Having never lost a case, this ruthless titan in the courtroom often compared herself to a shark in a shallow pond filled with wary minnows. She struck quick, hard, and without warning. Prosecuting attorneys found themselves licking their wounds and shaking their heads in wide-eyed disbelief, questioning how she had so easily eviscerated their *airtight* case.

With Judge Howell about to take the bench, Ryan gently nudged Lauren.

"Take a gander at what our Mensa client is doing."

Slumped over a piece of paper and armed with a blue marker, defendant Martin Maze scribbled like a toddler who had just discovered crayons. Rail-thin and high-strung, Maze had also proven to be unpredictable, needy, and belligerent, when not peddling small bags of candy bearing his initials. He was the consummate volatile client. Like a temperamental or even faulty piece of equipment, he had to be continuously monitored or *fixed*.

Lauren swiveled in her seat rather than interrupt Maze. *He looks horrid,* she thought.

Packing the visitor's gallery were the all too familiar faces of the media who followed Lauren like paparazzi stalking a celebrity, hoping for a misstep. Also in the courtroom were lucky spectators occupying the coveted seats allotted to the general public and members of the grieving family.

Hustling toward the judge's bench, the diminutive court clerk juggled a pile of files that almost toppled past her head. Standing on the two-step riser, she strategically arranged them like a dinner place setting.

Lauren rotated her chair to face forward, knowing what to expect next. "Here comes our five-minute warning," she said to Ryan.

"Please turn off all cell phones," the clerk announced from her mighty perch.

A beam of light from high above the judge's imposing bench glistened on the bronze surface. Bursting forth from behind a cloud, the ray illuminated the great seal of California. The rising, early-morning sun had radiated through the stained-glass window at just the right angle to reflect upon her. Summer in the City of Angels; an omen that Lauren Hill's brand of justice would be served. "We've got this," she mused.

But her euphoria ended abruptly. Looking at her pathetic sap of a client, she whispered to Ryan, "Get a handle on him."

Although the air conditioning provided a more than tolerable courtroom environment, Maze looked like a wet sponge being squeezed. The profuse sweat from his tightly wrinkled brow plastered his thinning hair to his head. Dressed in a tight-fitting, dark gray flannel suit, he tugged nervously at his collar while salty tears snaked their way from his cheek to the corner of his mouth. Disgusted, Lauren imagined the taste of bitterness on his tongue.

"He's coming unglued. It won't be long before—"

Head reeling, Maze motioned to Ryan in an unspoken cry for help. The young attorney poured his client a glass of water from the water pitcher on the table and quietly told him to calm down. "Get it together." Maze's hands shook profusely as he barely managed to pick up the glass. And with the jury watching from a distance, he spilled some of its contents onto himself. Trying again, he brought the glass to his pursed lips and guzzled.

Lauren shook her head as Maze bit his nails to the first knuckle. Under the table, his leg pumped a mile a minute. Maze had mentioned that he had not had a sound night's sleep in God knew when. But there was more. He had aged, somehow.

Leaning in close to her associate, Lauren said, "Tell him to wipe the sweat, but not the tears."

Fighting the smell of perspiration permeating from Maze,

Ryan complied and cupped his hand over his client's ear, relaying Lauren's command. Maze shot her an irritated expression.

Responding with a stern, unflappable gaze of her own, Lauren sent the message that she was not about to put up with weepy insubordination. Maze obediently began searching his pockets. Lauren thrust open her briefcase, pulling out a cloth napkin she always carried for just such an occasion. Purposefully and calmly, she slid it toward Maze.

With trembling fingers, Maze picked it up and wiped the numerous droplets away before taking another huge gulp of water.

"Good boy," Lauren murmured.

"All rise," shouted the bailiff in an authoritative voice. "The Honorable Susan Howell is now presiding."

A former district attorney, Judge Howell received high praise from both the defense and prosecution for being fair, polite, and respectful. The seasoned, white-haired jurist briskly entered the courtroom, taking her place in the high-backed chair while gesturing for everyone to be seated. "Mr. Bradley. My clerk has informed me that we have some housekeeping to take care of?"

District Attorney Dillon Bradley stood.

Bradley exemplified the phrase "eye candy." His blue suits and white shirts were impeccably pressed, his thick brown hair was always perfectly in place, and his body was lean from countless hours at the gym. Six foot and rugged, the forty-two-year-old was the complete package. Women swooned for him, and not merely because he drove a candy-apple-red Porsche 911. The way he smiled and paid attention made each one believe she was the only woman in the room.

"Yes, Your Honor. Just an oversight. When we adjourned yesterday, the court numbered one of our exhibits as the People's No. 4. It should be the People's Exhibit No. 5."

"So noted, Mr. Bradley. You may proceed."

Good looks aside, Bradley had amassed a distinguished record of being extremely tough upon the criminal element of Los Angeles County. But missing from his resume was a win against Lauren. He had been outmatched by her a dozen times.

Determined to break that cycle, he and his team had diligently prepared what he fervently believed to be a solid case against the embattled defendant. For him, no doubt existed concerning the guilt of Martin Maze. Bradley had interviewed the witnesses and read the reports. More importantly, he had read it in the defendant's face; the word *guilt* was practically tattooed onto the guy's forehead. Bradley recognized Maze to be a bona fide liar and a cold-blooded killer.

"The People recall Captain Lars Johansen."

Seated a few rows behind the District Attorney's table, Captain Johansen slowly navigated toward the witness box, where he had sat for most of the previous afternoon. Like a ship's ideal captain, the distinguished graying gentlemen sported a neatly trimmed beard. Multicolored bars fastened to the breast pocket of his company's navy-blue suit represented years of service to the fleet. Lauren pondered. *He looks like the* Titanic *captain who sailed the iconic vessel to her doom that crisp April evening in the North Atlantic. Is this stoic appearance a prerequisite for a cruise ship captain?*

With Johansen in place, Bradley gathered his notes and approached the witness. His line of questioning began with the captain reiterating his duties the day the alleged murder had taken place. As he spoke, Lauren studied the older gentleman's expressions.

"Now, Captain Johansen, underneath the ship, there are two," Bradley held up two fingers for emphasis, "two massive propellers, weighing approximately two tons apiece."

"That is correct."

Bradley continued, "These two gigantic propellers are always turning, spinning, and churning up the water like a giant, industrial blender."

His body language already screaming, Ryan clamored to object. Without redirecting her focus from the captain's tolerant expression, Lauren calmly dropped a helping hand to Ryan's knee, digging her nails in ever so slightly.

"Hold on. Not yet."

Reluctantly accepting, Ryan sat disappointed in his chair.

"Always?" Johansen questioned. "No . . . no, that would not be exactly correct."

Bradley surveyed the seasoned captain. "You are saying they don't always spin? They do not churn the water?"

"When they are in operation, certainly, if that is what you mean. When engaged, of course, yes. They rotate very rapidly."

"And for what purpose?"

Suppressing a chuckle, Captain Johansen answered, "Why, of course, to propel the ship either forward or backward through the water."

"So, when the boat is moving . . . " Bradley dramatically gestured with his hand mixing and churning, "they're spinning around, churning up the water like a giant blender."

"Correct."

Gritting his teeth, Ryan leaned toward Lauren, strongly suggesting she object to "all the blender crap." She did not respond. Ryan wisely kept his mouth shut and seethed. But needing some distraction, he locked his eyes on the chair on the opposite side of him.

Maze focused on a crinkled photograph depicting him and his wife standing on the bow of the cruise ship. Frozen in time, they held each other closely, smiling happily for a festive moment shortly before Amanda's death.

Where did it go wrong? Maze wondered.

Tilting his chair, Maze motioned for Lauren's attention. She had to decide whether to ignore her client and keep her eyes trained on the captain, or give in to this interruption. She chose the latter, only to be startled by her client's latest revelation.

"On her computer, she kept playing them all night, over and over again. I stopped it. I did—twice—but she just poured herself more wine and turned it back on, kept playing them and playing them."

Exasperated, Lauren interrupted. "What? What did she play?"

"Everything from country to heavy metal. Songs about suicide. Rascal Flatts, U2, Peter Gabriel, Slipknot, Ozzy. One depressing, kill-myself song after another."

Having heard enough, Lauren sat up in her chair, waving her right hand for Maze to cease, but he went on, soon catching the attention of Judge Howell.

"Ms. Hill. Is there a problem?"

Uncharacteristically embarrassed, Lauren answered no.

"Fine. Then I trust you will instruct your client on the rules of civility while court is in session?"

"Yes, Your Honor."

Reaching for her yellow pad, Lauren feverishly jotted notes for handling her client's newest disclosure. She resolved to save the information for impeachment arguments to counter any favorable character statements Bradley would try to enter into evidence. Along with testimony and other damaging evidence already brought out in discovery and before the start of the trial, Lauren had set in motion a not-so-pretty picture of Amanda Maze. Not fair? Perhaps. But all's fair in love and war, and this certainly was war.

Bradley inquired, "Your Honor, may I continue?"

Judge Howell nodded, and Bradley resumed his examination of the captain. "Now, let me ask you this, on the night Amanda Maze was pushed overboard—"

Before Bradley spoke another word, the barracuda in heels

launched from her seat, vehemently objecting to the DA's line of questioning.

"Sustained," Judge Howell exclaimed. "The jury will disregard."

Lauren sneered while Bradley kept his amusement to himself. He had known what he was doing; once a jury hears something, they cannot unhear it. The wily prosecutor pushed forward.

"Captain Johansen, were both two-ton propellers the size of this courtroom?"

Lauren stood. "Objection!"

"Overruled."

"It's an egregious exaggeration, Your Honor."

Judge Howell began to consider her request. But feeling the moment slipping away, Bradley seized the reins.

"Your Honor, if it pleases the court and the defense, I will kindly rephrase." Before receiving a reply, he quickly addressed his witness. "Captain Johansen, can you say the propellers of the ship you piloted that voyage were *approximately* the size of this courtroom?"

Expecting to hear an objection, the captain waited for a beat. "Well, ah, maybe combined," he said, panning from one end of the room to the other. "I'd say that is a fair estimate. Sure."

"Okay, now that we have established—"

Bradley waltzed around the witness stand long enough to shoot Lauren his own vicious sneer. In response, Lauren, pretending to adjust her teardrop earrings, mouthed *asshole*. Though scratching to respond with something equally vulgar, the prosecutor calmed himself and returned to his witness.

"Now, let me ask you, sir. Were those enormous, courtroom-sized propellers by anyone's estimation and definition, spinning . . . " He trailed off to stare down his brilliant opponent. The lion and hyena circled one another. His voice elevated. " . . . ON THE NIGHT MRS. MAZE WENT OVERBOARD?"

Both Lauren and Maze jumped out of their seats, and the

members of the jury gasped collectively. Maze exclaimed, "I loved my wife," while Lauren once again vehemently objected.

Judge Howell warned Lauren, "Control your client, Ms. Hill, or I will have the bailiff escort him out of the courtroom. Do you understand?"

Ryan took Maze by the arm and forcefully thrust him into his chair. Taking full advantage of the chaos, Bradley told the client to kindly answer the question. The jury sat up to listen intently.

"Well," Johansen began.

Shooting her client an angry face, Lauren exclaimed, "I still object, Your Honor!"

Johansen continued. "I would say, depending on the time she went—"

"OBJECTION. FOUNDATION."

"Sustained."

Bradley pressed. "Were they, Captain? Tell us. Were they?"

Overwhelmed, Captain Johansen sought direction from the judge. Unsuccessful, he answered.

"Well, we traveled a good portion of the night."

Lauren screamed, "OBJECTION!!"

Judge Howell banged her gavel and seized control. "Order. Order in this court." But neither the defense nor the prosecution paid attention.

Johansen finished. "Until we reached port in the morning."

The entire courtroom ruptured in *oohs* and *ahs*. Bradley folded his arms and stood smiling like a Cheshire cat.

Enraged, Lauren threw her hands up. "Your Honor."

"Quiet. Quiet. I will have none of this dissension in my court." The courtroom abruptly grew silent, though Judge Howell simmered. Breathing deep and fast, she continued. "Both counsel. Approach the bench. Now!" Not to be made a mockery of while presiding over such a high-profile case in front of the scrutinizing media, she needed to retake command of her courtroom.

Bradley's grin quickly dissipated. He followed Lauren, and the attorneys converged upon the bench like two jackals examining a fresh kill. Gritting their teeth, they jockeyed for position while Howell discreetly covered her mic. Lauren blinked, and Bradley jumped first.

"Your Honor, I am only attempting to establish—instead of the proposed, fantastical possibility that Amanda Maze swam a hundred nautical miles and enjoyed sipping banana daiquiris on some remote island—"

Lauren interrupted, "You don't have a body, you mor—" She barely held her tongue. "And, you do not have a single witness."

"Your Honor, it is reasonable to assume the victim."

"What victim? You have not proved there is one!"

Judge Howell figuratively stepped between them. "Hey, hey. Both of you. Cease."

Bradley interrupted, but Judge Howell did not let him continue.

"Did you hear what I said, Mr. Bradley? I said, enough."

Pushing her luck, Lauren interjected.

"Your Honor, the district attorney has not established a timeline nor introduced concrete, unrefuted evidence when the alleged act took place. Without such, how can he start to make a case—"

"Save it for the appeal, counsel. You know and I know those propellers chopped the girl into fish food," Bradley injected.

"Enough. I am going to say this for the last time. Either one of you opens your mouths again before I make a ruling and I will slap you with contempt. Do I make myself clear?"

Both attorneys acquiesced in silence.

"Excellent." After an intense beat, Judge Howell took her hand away from the mic and sat back. "Objection sustained." She slammed her gavel with a hard crack.

Steaming mad, Bradley marched briskly back to his chair where he nearly collided with his colleagues. Huddled together as if it were fourth and goal on their opponent's one-yard line, the three of them plotted their next move.

Lauren remained at the bench. "Is there anything else, counselor?" the judge asked.

Lauren stood in silence, staring straight ahead as if mesmerized. "Counselor?"

Standing awkwardly, Lauren saw before her not the robed Judge Susan Howell, nor an ordinary bench in a Los Angeles courthouse, but a kingly throne of solid gold decorated with the finest and largest gems. Lauren squinted to make out a bearded male figure dressed in the purest and brightest white robe.

CHAPTER TWO

L auren scanned her foreign environment, trying to decide whether this was an elaborate, twisted hoax or if she had somehow lost her mind. The throne room appeared immense. There were no walls or ceiling. Instead, in every direction, the floor beneath her shined bright, vivid green swirls, like an emerald sea of glass. The ground stirred with the slightest movement of Lauren's feet, sending the intricate configurations in motion.

"Lauren." He softly called her name.

In royal regalia sat the omnipotent Creator of the known and unknown universe. Looking indeed like a mighty and just ruler, the Supreme Deity wore a crown of pure gold adorned with vibrant gemstones of various shapes and sizes, each more brilliant than the last. Its weight and size alone could easily snap the neck of the strongest Olympic athlete.

Equally impressive was His form-fitting breastplate, which must have been fashioned from pure gold. Polished to a glorious sheen, it hurt Lauren's eyes to gaze upon it. And on His feet, he wore sandals etched in bronze with straps so thick they seemed immovable.

His sword was most outstanding. Tightly fastened to His waist, the weapon too was intricately etched with swirls and fancy lettering and covered in the finest of diamonds and jewels.

"Lauren." He called her name again.

In sync with the sound of His voice, seven leaf-shaped lamps of gold lit the throne room. They had neither light bulbs nor connecting cords to a power source of any kind. The holy light appeared to be originating from within the lamps themselves.

"Lauren." The Almighty's voice now echoed through the room.

Closing her eyes, Lauren hesitantly turned away from the bench. *This must be a dream.* She saw the courtroom frozen in time: Bradley huddled with his two assistants, Maze wrestling to open a bag of M&M's, and juror number three finishing sneezing. All humanity within the crowded room remained in a perpetual state of suspended animation. Rubbing her forehead, Lauren whispered, "I must be working way too hard."

"There is no reason to be scared."

With buckling knees, Lauren turned to face the Almighty.

"Do you not recognize who is speaking?"

"Judge Howell?" Lauren said, dismayed and confused by the unnatural—no, supernatural—surroundings. "Your Honor?"

"Whom are you calling, child?"

"Child?" Lauren appeared stunned.

He gazed upon her with the deepest affection.

"Who? What?"

"I AM. It is I."

Looking again at her unfamiliar yet glorious surroundings, Lauren stepped back. Her brain finally responded to this improbable situation. She had to escape. Vacate at once. But to where? Frightened, she stuttered, "How—"

"How? Am I not the God who created all things great and

small, seen and unseen? I am He. Do I not control time? Molecular space. The spaces between space, and . . . " He gestured behind her. "Behold, this courtroom."

Waiting patiently for Him to speak volumes of knowledge and wisdom, twenty-four elders sat in the throne room around a richly grained table crafted from a single piece of carved lumber. Their wrinkled brows and long, snowy beards adorned their chins. Each wore dazzling white robes and gold sashes similar to their Father's. Their gold and jeweled breastplates shined with luminescence brighter than the noonday sun. Their swords too were of spectacular beauty.

With the elders singing harmonious praises to the One, Lauren stood soundlessly before them. "Impossible," she deducted. She shook her head, unable to comprehend. A few feet in front of her, a fly stopped in midflight and remained suspended.

"Let me help you. So you may believe. Come closer."

The elders became silent. In that instant, the elaborate, kingly raiment God wore was replaced with apparel more befitting modern times. His robe changed to a buttoned shirt creased on each sleeve. The breastplate was now a tasteful black tie with a plain, shiny silver tie clasp. His sandals too were gone, replaced with high-end, dark leather shoes polished to a military shine. No crown. No sword. Nothing imposing or intimidating whatsoever.

"Is this satisfactory?"

Lauren now saw a man in his mid-fifties, pleasant and unassuming. Indeed, He appeared flesh and bone, but He remained a complex pattern of flesh and aura. A radiant brilliance originated solely from and through Him. God never ceased being God, never lost his commanding presence. Lauren found herself responding to his magnetic spirit.

"Focus, Lauren." And with a smooth, fluid movement, He tapped an index finger against his lower lip. "Come forward, my child."

He called me "my child?" Disbelieving, she ignored the command. Instead, she fixated on her pounding head. All her usual confidence had deserted her: she was as tongue-tied before Him as a one-l law student before a Supreme Court justice. She had to be imagining this. She didn't like to think that the mind of a shark like her could suddenly plunge into delusional fantasy, but the alternative was even more terrifying. Yet she felt compelled to heed God's divine will, even if it was just the result of an overactive brain in the throes of insanity.

"Maybe if I shut my eyes for just a moment, I'll—"

"Concentrate, Lauren. When you were four, and your mother gave you a can of spray string?"

That wasn't quite right. If He had told the story accurately, Lauren would have stayed silent, but His (intentional?) inaccuracy left her compelled to correct Him. "Silly String."

"Yes. Silly String. She let you spray her."

"And I laughed so hard I had to go to the hospital," she remembered.

"Only laughter was not the reason you were taken there."

Lauren did not respond.

"Your appendix ruptured."

"Yes. But how did you know? How did you know?"

"It's what it means to be All-Knowing."

Lauren stiffened. *Dear God,* she thought.

"I heard that," He said.

Sitting back, He smiled. Just then, a creature flapping the most beautiful four wings swooped down—its body in the likeness of a lion; its head that of an eagle. The being landed and moved upright on feet similar to man. But instead of talons, the creature displayed six toes at the end of thick, meaty legs.

Walking toward God, the being bowed low and presented Him a beautifully etched crystal glass filled with an unrecognizable concoction. But unlike the light red colors of strawberry, raspberry, or tomato, the drink appeared a darker, rich maroon, the shade of cherry or pomegranate, but with the consistency of a milkshake.

"A taste, my dear?" He gestured toward Lauren. "It is quite delicious, I assure you."

Although curious, Lauren shook her head. "No."

"Your choice." He signaled His indifference, sipping from the chalice. He then turned to Lauren.

She gasped. Six eyes, three on each side of His head, blinked randomly as the Being moved toward her. Lauren stepped back.

"Are you frightened, my child?"

Just then, the creature spread its wings and took flight. Speechless, Lauren watched it gracefully ascend, trying to track its path. Taking another sip from the glass, He again waved his index finger, motioning Lauren to step forward.

Gazing upon the ornate throne and its occupant, Lauren took a moment to compose herself. "You. You are God—God, *God!*"

He grinned. "Now you truly see Me?"

Lauren nodded mutely.

"And you can hear Me. Yes?"

"Yes," she murmured.

"Ah, but will you listen to Me?"

CHAPTER THREE

Placing her trembling hand against her tightened brow, Lauren tried to distinguish reality from fantasy. Feeling a pressure building in her scalp, she dreaded the arrival of her greatest weakness; migraines brought a crippling, pull-the-shade-and-leave-me-alone pain that often left her in tears.

God sensed Lauren's discomfort building. But He had an important, if not life-altering message to convey to her that was far more important than the inconvenience of a tension headache. He had the pain of an entire universe resting upon His shoulders. Her discomfort was inconsequential. Still, sensing her misery, and being merciful and compassionate, God decided it best to alter the course of the conversation slightly.

"Why are you fretting over trivial things, Lauren? What has prevented you from understanding the truth?"

The Almighty did not measure time. A day. A month. A thousand years. What did a few extra ticks of the clock matter? Had he not stopped the Earth from rotating on its invisible but assured axis? Hadn't He resisted annihilating man's home and all living things residing upon it? God controlled every moment, every nanosecond of time. And He controlled the present conversation with Lauren.

She tried to focus, but her headache pounced. As she squinted into the heavenly light, it became more difficult for her to concentrate.

"Your migraine. Does it not confirm this it is in fact real?" He gestured to the expanse of the vastness of His heavenly throne room. "Have you ever had one of them in your dreams?"

Come to think of it—no. Several times she had had troubling nightmares and had awakened with a painfully stiff neck she assumed to have been caused by falling asleep in an awkward, uncomfortable position. But during the dream itself? Surely not.

Lauren mused. *How is it I have never questioned it before? How did He know I even had a headache?* Ever the one to use deductive reasoning even under the most stressful circumstances, Lauren tried to rationalize despite the pounding inside her head. *Maybe, just maybe, I'm imagining this. Perhaps God is not seated before me and exists just within my tortured mind.*

"So you still struggle to believe?" God raised His right hand almost unnoticeably off the armrest.

If not for His words accompanying the smallest of gestures, a mere flick of his finger, Lauren would have thought nothing more of it. But the minuscule movement by the Almighty seemed purposeful. In a flash, her throbbing headache vaporized without the slightest evidence it ever existed.

"You do work too hard, Lauren."

Relieved that the pulsing sensation was now gone, Lauren gently touched her forehead.

"You are not getting enough oxygen to the most vital of organs, the brain with which I endowed you. I can touch the blood vessels in your brain and feel them constricting."

"Touch?" *He can touch my blood vessels?*

"Yes!" God beamed and answered Lauren's unspoken

thoughts. "What is there to marvel? Greater works than these you will come to know."

Lauren did not respond, deciding to reserve judgment.

God's countenance changed. "You are a clever one, Lauren. Aren't you?"

Clever? What?

God continued. "You have always been clever, though. Cleverness—one of those stock and trade instruments of the ego. Another one thought himself clever. I made him slither upon his belly." A calculated pause. "What else, huh? Let us bask in the ego to its last. Drink our fill from its glistening chalice. Shall we?"

Lauren listened in silence.

"Pretty. Self-reliant. Tough as, one might say, nails. And fool. Yes. Fool. Most appropriate. Do you agree with My choice of words?"

Uncomfortable and annoyed, Lauren struggled to awaken from her awful dream, snapping her fingers, pinching herself, commanding herself to wake up. Nothing brought her out of her present state.

Still standing on the swirling, emerald sea of glass with the twenty-four elders seated at the ancient table observing her from a distance, Lauren then approached the Almighty. "God?—God in Heaven?" she spoke aloud, trying desperately hard to come to grips with this situation and make sense of it.

"Focus, Lauren. Remember. Will you? Remember with Me?" He whispered, "Remember Sunday school? Can you recall your Sunday School?"

"Uh, a little."

"Do you bethink the Proverbs?"

She reached deep. But her tired mind did not grasp the meaning. The impromptu pop quiz flustered her. "No . . . no . . . maybe. Ah. I do not."

"Wisdom—to make one wise—instead of the alternative."

"Alternative?" she questioned.

Whispering, God answered, "The fool, Lauren."

"The fool?"

"The fool mocks goodness. The fool mocks justice. The fool mocks that which they know is right. Ah yes, you are the irrefutably clever child. But are you wise? She who has an ear, let her hear."

The elders nodded their agreement.

"Make no mistake; there is no middle ground. One either has true wisdom, or he is the corporal fool. Do you know which of the two you are?"

Lauren stood attentive, staring at the Lord. "Foolish," she repeated. Incensed by the insinuation, Lauren intended to speak her mind. And considering it a vicious attack upon her person—her sanity—God or no God, she answered with all the sarcasm she could muster. "I am clever enough to recognize you are going to tell me I am the latter of the two."

God might have chosen to be equally enraged by His subject's insolence. Instead, he glared at her, amused by her petulance.

"Fools take it upon themselves to be clever for the sake of humility, at the sake of righteous trust."

"God. I am not afraid of you."

"I am sure you are not. The fool fears Me not. Proverbs, Lauren. Proverbs."

Defiantly placing her hand on her hip, Lauren panned the room for an escape route. But to no avail. She replied, frustrated.

"Proverbs? Proverbs? Where is this going?

"6:16-19. Six things . . . six things I hate. And seven are detestable to Me."

Lauren wished nothing less than for this nightmare to be over and to return to the courtroom and her world in another dimension or parallel universe or whatever. But God compelled her to gaze at His magnificent splendor and carry on the improbable and ostensibly impossible conversation.

One by one, God recited the seven deadly sins.

"Pride."

Softly holding the tone long enough to echo throughout the chamber, the Elders sang the word, *"Pride."*

"Envy."

"Envy."

"Greed."

"Greed."

Lauren was sure that she had crossed from competency to insanity, but as with the migraine headache moments earlier, she remained powerless to halt God's recitation.

Please. Anything, anything but insanity. Make it stop.

"You're not insane, My child. Step closer."

Reaching out, Lauren touched God's shirt, which felt surprisingly soft and lush with a hint of starch. It was unquestionably something not from this world.

"Is the touch not real? Heed me. Heed my Proverbs. Wrath," God called.

The melodic tone of the elders intensified. *"Wrath."*

Unconsciously, she slipped her hand inside His sleeve and began stroking His arm under the wispy material.

"Laziness."

The elders sang louder. *"Laziness."*

Pliant flesh and, underneath, bone. Truly He had made man in His image. In a flash, however, He was not He any longer.

From a distance, she heard "Gluttony."

The elders sound resonated at an almost deafening sound. *"Gluttony."*

Just a hair's breath away from the point of no return, Lauren edged closer to the precipice. A mere whisper, the almost nonexistent fading away of divine verbalization. "Lust."

"Lust."

Lauren grasped. In her desperate attempt to comprehend the

incomprehensible, she began pawing under the robe. It was no longer God's vestment but the black robe of Judge Susan Howell.

"Counsel!" Judge Howell exclaimed, attempting to yank her arm away. "Have you gone mad?"

Lauren screamed, "WHY ARE YOU SAYING THIS TO ME?"

Concerned this might be an attack upon Her Honor, the bailiff sprang into action. Grabbing his holster, he rushed the bench.

Suddenly, Lauren snapped out of it, burying her head in her free hand, stunned by the loss of consciousness.

Judge Howell held her arm to stop the bailiff.

"Ms. Hill, I am asking you to kindly remove your hand and go back to your table."

Oh, gawd. Red with embarrassment, Lauren yanked her hand away from Judge Howell's robe and retreated to her table. The entire courtroom audience, including her client, stood and stared in shock. Ashamed and apologetic, she tilted her head meekly at Judge Howell.

"I'm s-sorry. I don't know—"

The judge lifted her gavel. "It is an understatement, a real understatement, to say we need to have a recess right now. Court will reconvene in one hour."

One hour, Lauren pondered. *One hour to regain my life.*

CHAPTER FOUR

L auren grabbed her briefcase and made a beeline out of the
courtroom. She did not even pause to acknowledge her
flabbergasted associate or client.

Her eyes welled with tears as she weaved her way past a
gauntlet of intrusive reporters anxiously following her. *Animals!*
Reporters might not have the sharp teeth and claws of predators,
but their digital recorders and nasty turns of phrase were just as
effective at tearing people apart. Lauren dealt with their cruelty
every day, but rarely was it directed at her. Shouts of "Ms. Hill,
can you tell us what just happened?" and "What made you lose
it back there?" rang out, as microphones were thrust at her.

Lauren needed to get away, if only for a few hours. Yes, that
would do it. That would be enough time to relax and collect her
thoughts. *Then I'll be okay. I'll be fine,* she thought. But Lauren
wasn't given that luxury. She only had sixty minutes to recover.

With newshounds hot on her tail, Lauren ducked into the
ladies' restroom and shut the door behind her. She leaned back
against the solid oak door and sighed.

A wispy lock of curly, blonde hair fell out of place, in front of her eye. Lauren walked to the first of three wash basins and gazed into the mirror. It was worse than she'd thought. Her normally impeccably styled mane was an untidy mess and the tasteful eyeliner she had applied earlier that morning was running down her cheeks. Tears ran down to her chin, bringing the chalky highlights with them. *I look like Alice Cooper,* she thought.

Lauren turned both faucets on and began running through her time-tested grooming techniques. Rifling through her attaché for emergency supplies, she went to work repairing the damage.

"What—what—what was that, damn it? What the hell just happened to you?" Lauren spoke aloud, not just scolding her bedraggled reflection, but also hoping beyond hope to find some rational explanation for the event which had just taken place inside the courtroom. Not surprisingly, the woman in the mirror had no answer. She just stared blankly back at herself.

Her outward appearance was returning to normal, but that wasn't the main issue. After washing off the old and applying the new, she still wasn't ready to face the ravenous mob she knew was still circling like lions around a wounded gazelle separated from the rest of the herd. She could hear them in the corridor just beyond the door. She was frustrated with herself for her actions in the courtroom. She began talking to herself, replaying the moments just before she blacked out.

Yes, that's exactly what happened. I blacked out! She remembered standing with that loser, Bradley, at the judge's bench, her inner kiln fired up as it did whenever she was really digging into a trial. Yes, certainly. *I was heated, and then . . . then I . . .*

Suddenly, the door opened and in walked a petite brunette. Reporters couldn't help peeking inside to catch a glimpse of Lauren. A guard stood in the hallway, allowing only court personnel to use the restroom. Otherwise, female muckrakers would have tailed Lauren into it.

"Savages," the woman said as she headed toward one of the stalls.

Lauren was instantly leery of the newest addition to the ladies' restroom, whom she had never seen before. However, to her pleasant surprise, the unknown brunette did not morph into the omnipotent Ruler of the Universe, or, worse yet, a reporter. She remained just a woman.

The brunette hurried into a stall, uncomfortably aware of Lauren staring at her. She shut and latched the door, resisting the urge to peek above it to see what Lauren was up to.

Lauren turned to look in the mirror once again. "Damn!" Those barely noticeable but, to her, unsightly wrinkles around her eyes were starting to show. The inevitable advancement of a woman's archenemy—age. Until recently, she had kept them at bay using her natural concoction of lemon juice, egg whites, and Vitamin E. But because she had been crying, they had surfaced as if emboldened. Lauren dug through her briefcase and brought out the big guns. She gently smoothed away the wrinkles with a dab of foundation.

She could see the older woman's feet from under the door reflected in the mirror. *Nice shoes, she thought. What am I saying? Okay, you're not going crazy, Lauren,* she rationalized. *Just a little overworked. Long hours, long case. Just a weeeee bit tired, that's all. Hang in there, Lauren, you're almost done.* She reached for a tube of lipstick—and dropped it. "Shit!"

Whoooosh! came the unmistakable sound of a toilet flushing.

"Well, it certainly can't be God, if she's using the toilet," she whispered.

The latch slid open, and the woman tentatively walked out. She started toward the sink to wash her hands, but thinking twice about it, decided it best just to leave the obviously disturbed woman to her own devices and give her plenty of space. Hastily, the woman straightened her skirt and bolted out the door.

Lauren turned to the mirror to apply her lipstick and make final adjustments. She had a crowd to face that remained huddled around the restroom door, thinking, *She has to come out of there sometime.* Warpaint back on, she was ready to face the gauntlet.

Although she was able to dodge most of them, Lauren answered a few, selective questions from the newshounds. *Hounds—a good name for them,* Lauren mused. *They are always snooping and sniffing around.*

CHAPTER FIVE

The courtroom rapidly filled with the befuddled masses, returning from what had to be memorable conversations over greasy burgers, salty fries, and iced fountain drinks. Within minutes, the room where many defendants had come to know their fate was filled. Court was back in session. Lauren and Ryan dutifully filed into the courtroom, flanking Maze. As Ryan and Maze took their seats, Lauren glanced up at the clock. *11:27.*

Her obsession with time had begun at an early age when her mother quietly slipped away from ovarian cancer. Lauren had been at the impressionable age of eleven. She was holding her mother's soft, withered hand and sobbing uncontrollably as the kindly woman who had given birth to her and nurtured her breathed her last in room 126 of City of Hope Hospital. She watched with profound sadness as her tumor-ridden mother hitched and exhaled long, drawn-out breaths, then, finally became still. Through her blurred vision, Lauren remembered looking up at three of a kind—5:55 PM. She had never forgotten it. From then on, Lauren had always been preoccupied with the infinite progression of time.

She had to have at least one clock in every room in her house.

Several rooms had multiple timepieces, strategically placed. In her eyes, one could never have too many. The constant, monotonous ticking, which would irk many and drive others to near madness, soothed her. Clocks gave her a sense of control, a sense that perfection was achievable. Without them, life would be meaningless to her; she would not have been able to function or accomplish much of anything.

Lauren sat holding her shoulders in perfect posture. She was poised and ready, anxious to get started and redeem herself from her earlier fiasco. Detecting no sign of the near mental collapse she had experienced at the bench an hour earlier, she was a primed tigress with hungry cubs to feed, ready to pounce at the slightest weakness.

Maze leaned behind Ryan toward his attorney. "Ms. Hill? See something disturbing?"

Immediately, Lauren's face drained of color. She looked around nervously. Nothing seemed amiss. God had not reappeared, but she wondered if Maze had been able to see the heavenly manifestation, as well.

"I mean is our case okay?"

Lauren didn't know whether to be relieved or worried. If Maze had also seen the mysterious transformation, would that not confirm she wasn't crazy? On the other hand, no one else in the room had run up to her, acknowledging how wonderful it must have been for God to reveal Himself and converse with her at such an intense moment. So it could easily mean that both she and Maze were closer to that unfortunate state of mental health than she wanted to acknowledge. She had already felt her excitable client was on the verge of a nervous breakdown from the very first time she spoke with him on the phone and agreed to take his case.

"Hey, hey, just relax, Maze," Ryan reassured him. "You're talking to the only woman in California history who has never lost a case."

"Yeah, but I'm a man who's never known sustained love and happiness," Maze countered. "Honestly doesn't matter to me anymore. Could care less whether they set me free or set me on fire. I guess I don't want people to think I could do something like that to my wife—or anyone. I only have my dignity left. That still matters to me."

"Maze. Sit there—hold your water," Lauren huffed. "They don't execute anyone in California anymore."

"Please rise," the bailiff called out in his deep baritone. He couldn't help looking at Lauren, studying to see if she was going to be a threat to the judge.

"Please be seated," Judge Howell said before stepping onto the bench. She seemed just as anxious to put behind her what had happened before the break. As creepy as Lauren's apparent breakdown had been, she still believed Lauren to be an exceptional attorney. Lauren was gritty and showed a great deal of tenacity and spunk. She even wondered whether Lauren's antics were some legal ploy. "Court is in session and will now come to order."

Lowering his voice to a whisper, Maze said, "Maybe I should testify."

With a single finger to her lips, Lauren cut him off. Maze took the hint and scooted his chair back. She watched her client adjust himself as the prosecution's next witness took the stand.

To Lauren's amazement, Dillon Bradley's young-gun assistant attorney, Jack Osterman, stood and took the floor to question the witness. *What is Dillon thinking,* she wondered. *I'm gonna eat him alive.* Aloud, she added, "Okay, let's see whatcha got, kid."

Jack Osterman was a rookie, just a few short months out of law school. He was intelligent enough and professional-looking in his three-piece suit, although the pinstripes reminded Lauren of Al Pacino in *The Godfather*. She had always thought Pacino was wrong for the part. It was evident that young Mr. Osterman was not quite comfortable speaking in front of a crowd or questioning witnesses. He didn't seem all that sure of himself. Sure, he had to get his feet wet sometime; but in her opinion, a criminal courtroom was not the place to test one's mettle. Cracking under pressure in a high-profile murder case could derail a career.

"Mr. Ross," Jack cleared his throat and straightened his tie. "You're head of security for the ship." He paused to look at his notes. "The *Magical Quest*."

Lauren chuckled, slightly.

"I am deputy security chief on board the vessel."

"And, the last time you were on the stand, you said that you—" Osterman read from his notes a second time. "'Didn't check my watch, but saw the first rays of sunlight had pierced the sky.'" He read like a child, pausing slightly between each word.

Lauren openly scoffed at the boyish amateur. He was making rookie mistakes, and she wasn't about to cut him any slack. Not so much as a cough was heard in the courtroom. Judge Howell banged her gavel and shot Lauren a disapproving look. Lauren acknowledged the chastening with a duck of her head, but she was anything but sorry. She intended to rattle the kid.

A little shaken by the outburst, the young Osterman glanced at Bradley, who simply gestured his continued approval. Jack checked his notes and continued a bit more fluidly.

"The meaning being it was early morning when the defendant had informed you that his wife," he paused, choosing his words carefully, "went overboard. Would that be correct?"

"Yes."

"So, it was the break of dawn when the defendant came to your cabin. And what did you—?"

"Excuse me, but that's not quite right, sir. Mr. Maze was brought to me by the on-duty officer. I actually met them on deck," the witness clarified.

"Okay, right. And when you met them on deck, would you please repeat for us the first thing the defendant said to you?"

"Sure," Ross answered. "He said, 'I believe my wife jumped overboard.'"

"When?"

"He wasn't really sure."

Lauren stood. "Objection."

"Sustained. Rephrase the question."

Maze was nervously fumbling in his pockets. His face was noticeably flushed, and it was becoming increasingly difficult for him to breathe. He groped in his pocket and removed used tissues and a small prescription bottle. His hand was shaking. Ryan inconspicuously glanced over.

Maze was struggling to open the cap on the tiny plastic bottle. Palms moist with sweat, he couldn't get enough of a grip on it to turn the childproof lid. Pills rattled in his shaky hand. Ryan looked over, rolled his eyes, and took the vial from Maze's hand. Effortlessly, he opened it and handed it back to Maze.

It wasn't the first time he'd had to intervene in one of Maze's crisis situations. Bouts of crying, courtroom outbursts, nervous twitching. Ryan was growing tired of his antics. He hadn't signed up for this. He hated being nothing more than a glorified babysitter. In law school, Ryan had never realized just how much non-lawyering there was to the job. He wasn't a psychologist.

To him, Maze was excessively nervous and sappy: a pathetic, hot mess. Did he believe the guy was innocent? He wasn't a mind reader. He didn't care one way or the other. It wasn't up to him to decide, anyway. That was a jury's job. However, the erratic way in which Maze was acting certainly made it seem as if he had a great deal to hide. More important, if Ryan had noticed flaws in Maze's character, it was very likely the impressionable jury would, as well. All he knew for certain was that Maze was making it difficult for Lauren to paint a picture of innocence.

Ryan leaned over. "The pills. What are they for?"

Without looking up, Maze said, "Triggers."

"What triggers?"

"Like wanting to turn off my mind, you know, and just be with her again. We all have the same triggers of grief; we just don't all have the same capacity to deal with them."

Osterman continued. "When you asked Mr. Maze when he thought his wife jumped overboard, what was his reply?"

"I think he said—"

"Think or know?" Osterman interrupted.

Lauren noted that the kid's line of questioning was getting better, but she knew, sooner or later, Jack Osterman was going to slip up. And when he did, she would be ready. For now, though, she could give him kudos.

"I believe—"

"Would you like me to read from your prior testimony? Allow me to—"

"Thanks."

Osterman read from his notes, "I quote, 'Mr. Maze looked like he didn't expect me to ask such an obvious question and then, after a long stare away from looking at me, that is, he simply said he wasn't sure because he hadn't seen her all night.' Now, was that accurately your original testimony?"

"It was."

"*All night?* Did you find that particularly odd?"

"Well, yes. Certainly."

"And when you asked Mr. Maze where he was, what was his reply?"

"Until the crack of dawn? According to him, he left the casino at five-fifteen."

"That would be five-fifteen in the morning?"

Of course, five-fifteen in the a. m., you twit, Lauren thought. *That's when dawn is. Get to the point.*

"Yes," the deputy security chief replied.

"And was this verified?"

"Yes," Mr. Ross replied.

At the defense table, Lauren leaned toward Ryan. "Look at him. He's almost as much of a sap as Maze, a rank amateur. Copying Bradley's style. He's got his head so far up Bradley's ass, I'll bet that every time he farts, the kid's ears wiggle."

Ryan was barely able to contain his laughter.

"Miss Hill?" Maze interrupted.

"Dealers, waitresses?" Osterman questioned.

"Yes, sir."

Maze had popped a couple of pills from his vial and was leaning past Ryan, trying to get his lead lawyer's attention. Lauren had kept ignoring him, elbowing Ryan to keep Maze under control. Finally, she responded.

"What pills are you taking, and what do you want?"

"I want to testify."

"I don't want you taking anything while we're here. Do you understand? You have to look alert. Zombies fry. And I'll decide when or if you testify. Now sit still."

"I have told everyone the truth."

"I know, I know. We'll talk about it later. For now, just do as you are told. Got it? Pay attention to what's happening on the witness stand."

Their eyes shifted toward Osterman, who continued his scripted questioning. "Would it still have been dark outside?"

"Objection."

Dillon Bradley shot out of his chair. The kid had performed well, but he was a bit out of his league, and Dillon knew when to take over.

"We have a chart, Your Honor."

CHAPTER SIX

What constitutes a fair trial? It usually depends upon which side you ask. Ask one hundred different individuals, and you will likely get one hundred different responses.

Dillon Bradley simply wanted to see justice carried out. For him, it wasn't how many checkmarks were in the *win* column, although that did matter to the voters in November. Grieving parents wanted answers, and he believed they deserved to have them. He also believed he and his team would be able to provide them, or at least a majority of the important ones. A guilty verdict would, in theory, clear most of them.

As flawed as the law could sometimes be, Bradley believed the American justice system was the fairest in the world. Granted, he realized the evidence in the present case was somewhat sketchy; however, he honestly believed he had enough to sway a jury and get a conviction.

For Lauren, on the other hand, it was all about winning. She never took a case based on whether she believed in her client's innocence. She didn't take one because she was defending a tarnished honor. That was irrelevant to her. She took it based solely on the evidence provided. If she believed the prosecution would not be able to prove beyond reasonable doubt the accused's guilt, the system worked. All must, by law, be represented and offered a fair trial, and since that was the case, Lauren Hill gave it everything she had. Getting paid handsomely to do so sweetened the deal.

Lauren saw her performance in court as a game of strategy, a chess match. She dressed the *king,* the defendant, putting him or her in the best possible light, and then stood like a *knight* in front of him, defending the accused to the very best of her ability. She had a perfect record to uphold. Was it realistic to think it would remain perfect throughout her entire career? Certainly not. It was her job to put off the inevitable as long as she could. And right or wrong, it was her feeling that she wasn't going to lose this one, either. But she had to admit her opponent was formidable. Could she beat Bradley yet again?

Bradley crossed the floor, carrying a large timeline graph. He handed it to Osterman to set it up, but not before complimenting the young protégé on the fine job he had done. While Jack set up the chart, Bradley told the court to strike Osterman's previous question.

Lauren sat tensed, ready to pounce.

Bradley began, "Your Honor, I would like to submit into evidence this chart: a timeline of sunrises and sunsets for the latitudes and longitudes of the week of the fateful cruise, specifically, the last day Mrs. Amanda Maze was seen alive."

"I will allow. Please, continue."

Lauren leaned over to Ryan and mockingly mouthed *yippee* to him. He chuckled. She glanced at Maze. He was still fidgety but silent. Out of the corner of her eye, she could swear God was sitting at the bench giving her a stern look, but when she turned, it was only Judge Howell staring at her, eyebrows raised in stern warning. Lauren sat up and faced forward.

Turning to the deputy security chief, Bradley asked, "Mr. Ross, can you see this chart well enough?"

Ross answered in the affirmative.

"It's a graph that marks the times of sunrises and sunsets the week of the cruise. The time of the sunrise on the day Mrs. Maze was last seen is in red. Can you see this?"

"Yes."

"What time does it say the sun rose the morning you spoke to Mr. Maze?"

Squinting, Ross answered, "Six twenty-three."

"Six twenty-three, yes, thank you. So, it must have been somewhere within forty-five minutes to an hour, at the latest, between the time Mr. Maze, by witness account, left the casino and the time you spoke with him on deck, correct?"

"Yes, I suppose so."

"And did you ask him to account for the time?"

"Yes, yes, I did."

"Where did the defendant say he was for that short duration?"

Maze, under his breath, said, "Lost on deck during the fog."

"He didn't."

"He didn't? What do you mean, he didn't? He must have said he was somewhere."

"Just that he was lost on the ship."

"Lost?" Bradley chuckled. "Isn't it rather difficult for one to get lost on a ship?"

Everyone—reporters, spectators, lawyers—snickered. All, that is, except the parents of the deceased. Unable to bear the mocking laughter, Maze jumped up.

"It was foggy. I was lost in it trying to find the cabin. I loved my wife. I loved her. You don't kill what you love!"

Judge Howell stood, furiously banging her gavel, as Ryan practically tackled him.

"ORDER! ORDER IN THE COURT! MR. THOMPSON AND MS. HILL—PLEASE—" Judge Howell paused.

Ryan assertively ushered Maze to the back of the courtroom and the exit. Bradley folded his arms, exceptionally pleased with himself.

"—CONTROL YOUR CLIENT!" Judge Howell bellowed.

"Yes, Your Honor," Lauren offered.

Amused by the way Ryan was holding onto the back of Maze's jacket, as if he were throwing outside a dog that had snuck into the house and soiled the carpet, the armed deputies at the rear of the courtroom opened the doors ahead of them. Once Ryan and Maze were outside, the guards, grinning widely, quickly closed the doors. Lauren was now alone and in her comfort zone. For a few moments anyway, she was in her element and could focus her attention solely on the proceedings.

Bradley's Cheshire cat smile didn't amuse the judge. "If you're through grinning, Mr. Prosecutor, you may continue any time you are ready."

Ryan Thompson was furious with Maze, and as he talked to him in a barely controlled voice, his face was flushed and his forehead wrinkled. Had he not been in a professional setting and his job not depended upon him keeping his cool, Ryan would likely have decked the guy. Maze's untimely explosion had not only made him look foolish in the eyes of the court and jury, but it had also put the defense team fighting for him in a poor light. Now Lauren was going to have to scramble. Bad enough she was obviously under a great deal of stress as it was. Maze's only job was to sit quietly and remain composed. If he could not do so on his own, it was up to his defense team to make sure he obeyed all guidelines. Maze's frustrated tirade had done him no favors. The only things Maze had accomplished were to anger Judge Howell, make the jury believe he was unstable, and give Prosecutor Bradley an upper hand.

"We've told you before, you cannot spout off like that. What don't you understand? The only logical conclusion a jury can make when you pull a stunt like that is you're uncontrollably angry, a loose cannon. You don't want them to believe you killed your wife."

Maybe it was just the way he had phrased it, but to Maze, it sure sounded an awful lot like Ryan believed he did kill Amanda.

"I didn't kill my wife," Maze repeated, grabbing Ryan by the collar. "Listen, I've been in and out of that room for days, and I'm being dissected like a rat in a science lab."

"Look!" Ryan ripped Maze's sweaty hands away from his shirt. He straightened his jacket and gave Maze a death stare.

Immediately, Maze transformed into an ashamed puppy who soiled the rug. He even whimpered. "I'm sorry, I'm sorry, man."

Unrelenting, Ryan continued to pour it on. "Pull yourself together, NOW! You hear me? Let me tell you something, buddy. Lauren Hill is in there fighting her ass off for you. She has never lost a case, NOT ONE, and she has no intention of losing this one. But you're doing a good job all by yourself. You know the drill. This is a lengthy process. As unfair as you or I or anyone else might think it is, this is the system of law."

"This isn't what I call law. It's an inquisition. That's what it is. They—"

"Hey—HEY. What the hell is your problem? Is it those pills?" Ryan pointed to Maze's jacket pocket. "Gimme those!"

Quickly, Ryan reached into Maze's coat pocket as Maze tried to wriggle away. Like an old Abbott and Costello skit, the two comically wrestled for the prescription bottle. Only no one was laughing. After a short tussle, Ryan rattled the bottle of pills in front of Maze.

"These new pills?" Ryan held Maze at arm's length while he carefully read the label. Maze didn't fight him. Seeing all he needed to, Ryan tossed them back to him.

"I want to testify," Maze said, juggling the pill bottle with his unsteady hands. As if addicted, he carefully tucked it away inside his pocket and patted it.

"Yeah, and say what, huh? What could you say that they don't already know from the police interrogations and the physical evidence? Ms. Hill has already had this conversation with you several times. Unless there's something else we should know?"

Maze clammed up. He didn't like what the hotshot attorney was insinuating. He didn't like it at all. It was the second time in about as many minutes he had seemed to imply that Maze had something to confess. He stood silently staring back at Ryan. For the first time, it appeared Maze had absolutely nothing to say.

Ryan looked deep into Maze's eyes. He couldn't pinpoint it, but something didn't seem right to him.

"Well, are we good? Are we clear? You're not testifying, got it? It's not the best play."

"But Ms. Hill said—"

Ryan blurted, "That was just to get you to shut the hell up about it in court!"

Not happy, Maze saw he had only two options, and one of them would not produce the results he wanted. He had no other recourse but to agree.

Ryan toned down, trying to calm his client. "Now, look, let's get back in there and sit quietly. Okay?" He gently shook him. They were pals for the moment.

Maze looked him in the eye and nodded. The two started to make their way into the courtroom.

"Ryan?"

"Yeah."

"Thanks, it's been really tough, you know. Really tough."

"I'm sure it has." Ryan clasped Maze on the shoulder, much less forcefully going in than coming out. He walked his client through the door and back to his seat.

CHAPTER SEVEN

Dillon Bradley rubbed the laughter away from his tired eyes. Naturally, Lauren hadn't found it amusing in the least and scowled at him. *Just get on with it, shall we, Mr. Prosecutor?* she thought.

Jury members leaned into one another, conversing amongst themselves. Ravenous reporters made entries in their portable tape recorders or jotted detailed notes as fast as their fingers could fly across the pages. Few in the room had no opinion one way or the other on what had taken place. Some saw an innocent man fighting for his life, while others saw instability.

Not letting things get too far out of hand, Judge Howell banged her gavel repeatedly. Murmurings from the gallery of stunned courtroom observers slowly died down. Once the room was entirely quiet, Bradley continued questioning the witness for the state.

"Where was I? Oh, yes—Mr. Ross, did Mr. Maze know where his wife was?"

"Objection!"

The judge was quick to overrule. Turning to the witness, she told the deputy security chief he needed to answer the question.

"He said he didn't know."

"So, let me get this straight, by the time you reached Mr. Maze on the bridge, he claimed he had been lost, wandering around aimlessly in the fog, and didn't know where his wife was. However, according to the defendant, he last saw her in their cabin, where he admitted they had an awful fight, just before he left for the casino and gambled for the next five hours or so. At this point, on deck all these hours later, Mr. Maze coolly claimed that he believed his wife had gone overboard. And yet he came to this conclusion without having taken the time to look for her."

Lauren jumped from her chair, slapping her hand on the table for effect. "Objection!"

"Overruled."

"Does this summarize what the defendant told you?"

"Yes. Yes, it does."

At just this crucial moment, Maze reentered the courtroom, followed closely by Ryan. Light murmuring commenced as everyone stared, scrutinizing his every move while taking mental notes. Judge Howell banged her gavel three times in rapid succession but said nothing. The courtroom quieted. All watched in silence as Maze took his seat.

Bradley continued. "Mr. Ross, did the defendant say if he bothered to look for her, or not?"

Angered, Lauren bolted out of her seat.

"Objection! Is this a circus? Should we bring in the clowns?" A wisp of hair floated down in front of her eyes, and she purposely shook her head and blew it aside.

The courtroom immediately ruptured in laughter. Enraged by Laurel's inappropriate outburst, Judge Howell banged her gavel. "Reluctantly sustained. Ms. Hill, I'm warning you."

Although he had lost that battle, Bradley thanked the judge and continued. "Mr. Ross, did you at any time ask Mr. Maze if he had looked for his wife?"

"Yes, I did."

"And what did he say?"

"He said he did."

"Were you able to verify that claim?"

"Objection."

"Overruled."

Lauren was piqued, but not frustrated to a great extent. Her every move was calculated, a theatrical masterpiece. She sat glaring intently across the room at Judge Howell. *So far, so good.* The judge hadn't morphed into God, or anything else, for that matter. She still had her sanity—for the time being, anyway. Judge Howell felt Lauren's eyes burning into her and curiously stared back.

"So then, are we to conclude that no one—no one—confirmed his assertion of searching for her?"

"No, not to my knowledge, but it was quite early in the morning. Most if not all of the passengers on board were asleep at that time."

"And what was the defendant's demeanor? Upset? Scared? Anxious?"

"OB-JEC-TION!" Lauren shouted. Now she was fuming, drumming her fingers impatiently upon the edge of the table and tapping her foot, loudly.

Before the judge could offer a ruling, Prosecutor Bradley was on top of it. He instantly rephrased the question.

"In your *opinion*, Mr. Ross."

"Fairly calm."

"Calm," his star witness said.

"Calm. As calm as the defendant appears to be now?"

"Much calmer."

The son-of-a-bitch killed his wife, Bradley thought, *and he was calm about it—calm! And it's not like he just has a naturally*

*calm disposition, if the last few damn days are any indication!
I wasn't sure before, but I am now. I want this guy to fry, but
since that can't happen in this state, I want him to never again
see the light of day. Not this time, Lauren. I'm gonna get him.*

Bradley turned to smirk at Mr. Maze. Maze knew the crafty
prosecutor wanted him to react. With everything he had, Maze
averted his eyes.

Then Bradley looked at Ross and gazed deep into him. For a
moment, they fixed their eyes on each other like two grappling
rams, until . . .

Speaking aloud his previous thought, Bradley turned to the
court and said, "Calm? Calm? He believes his wife had taken the
plunge and yet . . . he's calm?"

Maze spoke to himself, poignantly, staring blankly through
Mr. Ross. But in the quiet of the interior courtroom, many heard,
"Not true. Not true. You told me not to panic, to remain calm.
You made me remain calm."

The defense, the jury, the prosecution, the witness, and, most
importantly, Judge Howell heard Maze's comment. She briefly
went for her gavel, raised it, and then, deciding not to stir up
even greater mockery, silently lowered it to the bench. Much to
Bradley's chagrin, the judge opted to take the high road and let
the unsuitable remark slide for the time being.

Ross nervously adjusted himself in his seat. Suddenly, he felt
warm. He placed a forefinger under his tight-fitting collar and slid
it down to the first button of his shirt. It felt as if it were digging
into his Adam's apple.

"Well, to answer your question, the captain and I did in fact
reassure Mr. Maze and recommended he remain calm, that we
would perform a sweep of the entire vessel. In most cases, we do
find the lost somewhere on board."

Bradley was clearly frustrated with the deputy chief's answer
and looked over to the defense table. Lauren leaned back in her

chair and folded her arms, noticeably pleased. Bradley quickly turned to attempt a different approach.

"Would you please tell the court what Mr. Maze uttered when you asked him why he thought his wife went overboard instead of still being on the ship?"

"Certainly. He kept repeating he loved her, many, many times."

"Is that all the defendant said?"

"No, no. He followed those assertions with something about her being bipolar and that they had had a very heated argument. He said she had threatened to jump."

"So, Mr. Maze said he loved her, but didn't check on her all night, and—"

Lauren jumped from her seat. Maze's instinct was to do the same, but Ryan was ready. He responded to the first sign of movement and quickly gripped the man's arm. Ryan squeezed tight. Maze settled in his chair.

"Objection!"

Maze leaned over to Ryan and began to speak. "I did love—" but Ryan held up his hand, in warning, to prevent him from finishing his sentence. Lauren was already on top of it and didn't need the judge banging the bench for her to contain her unstable client. Lauren harshly objected a second time.

Although far from pleased with the defendant's unruly behavior, Judge Howell had no choice but to sustain the request and tell the jury to disregard the unfinished question and any drawn inferences.

Bradley was momentarily flummoxed but, looking down at his notes, quickly recovered and moved on to his next question.

"Isn't it true, Mr. Ross, that in your initial investigation, you found a partial bloody palmprint on a pane of glass on the balcony, blood which was later analyzed?"

"Yes."

"And whose was it?"

"It was found to be that of Amanda Maze."

"No further questions, Your Honor."

Lauren stood, ready to seize the moment. She turned to briefly give Maze a reassuring pat on the back for all to see. He smiled. Clearly, the kind gesture meant a great deal to her weary and befuddled client. He looked up and seemed to relax, knowing it was her turn to go on the offensive.

Judge Howell looked at the witness. "You may step—" she began.

"Wait! I'm sorry," Bradley interrupted. "Mr. Ross, would you please remind us how the balcony door looked to you when you first saw it."

"Yes. It was broken, shattered into hundreds, if not, thousands of fragments."

"That's right. I almost forgot. That's all, thank you."

"If that is everything," Judge Howell gazed toward a retreating prosecutor. Bradley glanced up and acknowledged it was. "You may step down, Mr. Ross."

Lauren scoffed at Bradley's perfectly timed display of forgetfulness and stepped lively toward her opponent, muttering, "Grandstanding piece of shit."

Bitch! Bradley thought as he turned toward his seat.

Lauren stepped toward the witness stand and then turned away as if to say *Never mind.* Maze stared at his defense attorney, mouth agape. He was wondering why she had chosen not to cross-examine the witness.

Of course, Lauren knew exactly what she was doing. She waited until the witness had nearly cleared the box before saying, "Wait, Mr. Ross, I have just one question."

CHAPTER EIGHT

L auren was ready to explode Bradley's examination of the
security officer with one question that would require a
simple *no* reply.

She had known what to ask Ross even before her client had
ruptured a gasket and been ushered out the back door. The
only question left for her was, *Will the jury remember Maze's
outburst and hold it against him, or will they remember Mr.
Ross' answer?*

Grinning widely, Lauren sauntered up to the witness box. She
tapped a glimmering, high-heeled shoe on the floor and turned
to face the witness who had retaken his seat.

"Mr. Deputy Security Chief, I have but one question to ask
you," she said in her sultry voice, which had brought many a
man to his knees, including her docile husband. She took a long
pause as if considering how best to word the question. It had to
be worded correctly, stated precisely in such a way as to get the
desired response. Then she acted as if it had suddenly come to
her. Of course, this was all for dramatic effect.

"Mr. Ross, after performing your on-board investigation,

do you have any material reason to believe that anything—
anything—Mr. Maze told you that morning was less than one
hundred percent truthful that is, based solely upon only *your*
investigation?"

Mr. Ross looked to Bradley for help and received it.

"Objection."

"Overruled."

Lauren smiled at Ross and waited for his reply. Finally, almost
inaudibly, he said, "No."

"Would you repeat that a little louder for the court, please?"

"No!"

Murmuring commenced, both among the members of the
jury and the spectators at the back of the room. Bradley sat back
in his chair, frowning.

"No further questions, Your Honor."

"Now, the witness may step down."

Like the hen highest on the pecking order, Lauren puffed
herself up and strutted with newly regained confidence back
toward her seat. She didn't notice, but the top three buttons on
her sheer blouse strained to keep her neatly tucked into place.
Lauren showed her most convincing death stare to Bradley as
she walked past, but it was lost on him. Dillon's eyes were overtly
riveted just a tad bit lower than were hers.

Black bra. Damn, Dillon thought. He craved, desired, coveted,
and yes, lusted!

Lauren looked down to where Bradley's eyes were focused and
gently tugged her blouse back into place. *All pigs,* she thought.
She reached her table and spun around to face the judge.

Once again, Judge Howell was transformed.

Oh, no. Not again!

Lauren's expression transformed into one of fear. Somewhere
beneath her cranium, an alarm went off. Her body became rigid
as the same unwelcome sensation gripped her. She froze.

God was staring back at her from the bench from within the black justice's robe of Susan Howell.

Lauren did a double-take, paused, and looked again. "Please, let it not be real," she whispered to herself.

But it was all too real. The neatly trimmed white beard, wrinkled brow, and stern countenance were undeniable. The glaring figure of God. She slowly glanced around the cavernous room. It seemed larger, but at least this time, it was still a courtroom. As normal, whispered conversations were taking place.

Bradley was in conference with his team, plotting their next move; reporters were bickering amongst themselves; a few jury members were in deep discussion about what to make of Mr. Ross's answer.

Lauren needed to avert her eyes and turned to her left. Ryan was beaming up at her with a congratulatory, almost worshipful smile. No one else seemed to notice Judge Howell's metamorphosis.

Suddenly, Lauren dashed toward the clerk and grabbed the Bible used for swearing in off his desk. Without opening it, she raced back to the table. Conversations ceased as everyone turned to look once again at the crazy attorney.

Lauren's head was reeling. The walls seemed to be rapidly closing in on her. Although she was no longer looking up at Him, Lauren could feel God's burning presence glaring down at her and through her. She began to hyperventilate. Then, in a state of sheer panic, she spotted it. Instinctively, she raced to Maze's side of the table and snatched his bottle of anxiety medication. Opening the cap, she dumped all the pills into her hand. Ryan reached out to stop her. Too late. Lauren thrust a pill into her mouth, dry swallowed, and dropped the rest.

Maze scrambled. He tried to retrieve his medication before the yellow tablets rolled off the table. His meaty little hands were able to corral most of them, but several slipped past. He dove to the floor to recover them.

As Maze scooped the prized possessions back into the vial, Lauren bolted to the rear of the courtroom and out the back door, leaving a packed courtroom stunned.

In wide-eyed astonishment, Ryan threw his hands up and looked to the judge for some guidance. Judge Howell stood and told him to go after her.

Lauren was frantic. Her breathing was elevated to a near frenzy, and she was starting to foam at the mouth. Lauren splashed herself with water from the drinking fountain as if she were on fire, as if the cold water might bring her back to reality. Plenty of people saw her anguish, but none stopped to offer assistance. Many believed it was just another psycho woman in a city which seemed to produce far too many crazy beauties. They stood aside, giving her a wide berth.

Turning away from the drinking fountain, Lauren took the Bible and began rifling through the pages.

Catching up to her, Ryan clutched her shoulders, more for his own safety than as a way of helping her. He had no earthly idea what she was capable of in such a state. Quickly, he spun her around to face him. He shook her, trying to snap her back to reality. She scared him. Her eyes were wide with either fright, mental illness, or an undetermined combination of the two.

The Bible slipped from her fingers and fell to the floor. Lauren watched as it fluttered open. She reached down to retrieve it, but Ryan prevented her from doing so. In his strong hands, she began to tremble, and then shake. She was on the verge of passing out. She held a hand to her mouth and pointed. No longer did she have to search for what she was seeking. On the floor by her right foot, facing up as if accusing her was the book of all books opened to Proverbs. Highlighted in yellow was the verse 6:16!

As he tried to hold her upright, Ryan's grip tightened. "Oh, my God, Lauren! Get a hold of yourself!"

At the word *God*, Lauren regained the power of speech. She stood bolt upright, grabbed Ryan's suit sleeves. "You saw Him, too?"

"Who, Lauren?"

A small crowd of men had gathered around, unsure whether to deck Ryan for accosting the beautiful damsel or assist him in hauling her away. They stood silently, waiting to hear more.

"The judge. Did you see Him?"

"Him? Her? You mean Judge Howell?"

Lauren began shaking her young partner by the shoulders. "Yes, damn it. Did they look different?"

Ryan shrank from Lauren; her eyes were ablaze and spittle formed at the corners of her mouth.

"How? In what way?"

Satisfied she was the crazy one, the crowd slowly dispersed without uttering a single word. Realizing Ryan hadn't seen what she did, Lauren released him.

"Never mind."

"Look, Lauren, I have no clue what you are talking about, but we have got to get you back in there. Howell is pissed, and rightfully so. Bradley and those yahoos are practically rolling in their seats. They're having a grand old time, and the bailiff is guarding Maze, who, like you, kinda seems to be unraveling at the seams. I need you to be you!"

Ding! Lauren's cell phone.

It was what she needed. The most minuscule of things brought her back from the brink. Lauren pulled her cell out of her suit pocket and glanced at it. It was a simple, one-word message: "Sex?"

CHAPTER NINE

Lauren Hill and her young protégé were huddled together just outside the courtroom entrance. She was making a few last-minute adjustments to her hair and garments while preparing mentally to face whatever punishment might befall her. Ryan stayed by her side, not only for moral support but to act immediately if Lauren showed any signs of breakdown. Her behavior was incomprehensible. What had befallen his boss over the course of the last few hours was unprecedented. Frankly, he was disgusted, but he also couldn't help but feel sorry for her.

Replaying several worst-case scenarios in her mind, Lauren prepared herself for everything short of being banished from the kingdom. What she had done, in the eyes of the court, could easily be considered grounds for disbarment. However, her exemplary track record, she honestly believed, would keep her from that fate.

She knew Judge Howell very well, yet there were no guarantees and realized she was in jeopardy of being handed serious reprimands.

How in the world would she be able to respond to the allegations? Tell Judge Howell she had witnessed her transform into God? That would fly about as far as a pregnant rhino in a light breeze. And what did she expect in return for revealing such truth? How ironic: she was a high-powered attorney getting paid rather handsomely to mislead or at least distort the facts enough to where they became truth. Yet if she were to go in there and tell what she damn sure believed had happened, there'd be a mistrial and she'd get a one-way ticket to Happy Acres.

Lauren kept replaying the strange events over and over in her mind. She honestly didn't believe she was slipping into the realm of lunacy. *Damn it to hell! What I saw was real!* She wasn't ready for basket weaving 101 or playing checkers until sunset. She was a lawyer, the best, and there was serious work to do.

Lauren and Ryan's main concern, of course, was damage control. She was wondering how she was going to turn an unforgettable situation around and make things right. *Not likely,* she thought. He was thinking about presentation—how to put himself in the best possible light and help his bedraggled employer save face. Neither seemed likely, and he was on edge.

Lauren glanced at her elegant Rolex, which informed her it was 12:37. *Ugh!* With the early lunch break, the day was dragging along far more slowly than she had expected. *Or does God somehow have His grubby hands on the flow of time, as well?* she wondered.

She wasn't being sarcastic. She had already witnessed the impossible stoppage of time performed by the omnipotent Ruler of the universe. It was certainly not beyond His abilities. But unless God revealed to her it was exactly what He was doing, she had no way of knowing.

Looking at Ryan, Lauren smiled shakily, trying to convey confidence. From his worried expression, she knew he wasn't buying it. Lauren took a deep breath and exhaled hard.

"Well, time to face the music, I guess."

"I know."

"Face forward and don't look intimidated," Lauren instructed. "They're vultures waiting to pick over the dead." Seeing his blank expression, she added, "Don't worry, it will all work out in the end."

Ryan wished he could believe that. Reluctantly, he opened the door for Lauren, and the two of them entered.

As they walked briskly down the center aisle, they could feel all eyes were upon them. Following Lauren's cue, Ryan remained focused on reaching their desk. They heard the murmurings, but neither of them gave the ravenous dogs of the press the satisfaction. Quietly, they took their places, and the bailiff backed away from Maze.

Judge Howell glanced up to acknowledge their presence, but she only nodded. Sure, she understood what pressure Ms. Hill was under to perform. But Judge Howell also had a duty to perform for the people of California. Thousands of taxpayer dollars had already been spent on the trial. In her eyes, the only recourse, for now, was to allow it to continue. It was too close to being in the books. Besides, before putting on her judge's robe, Susan Howell was first a woman. She knew firsthand what it was like to claw through a man's world. She commended Lauren for her string of successes and was rooting for her all the way. Still, she realized she couldn't let the usually bright attorney get away with any further interruptions. Delays were costly, both administratively and professionally. If she wanted to be reelected and remain on the bench, and she did, she had to consider the possibility of reprimanding Defense Attorney Hill. She would have plenty of opportunities to discuss Lauren's bizarre behavior with her in the near future, but for now, she decided to table it.

Bradley, for all his determination and smugness, looked concerned for Lauren when she returned to her place. Usually, he would have been gloating watching an opponent crumble, worthy or otherwise.

But this was the great Lauren Hill. It was so unlike her to falter. What she had done wasn't a simple fumbling for words, nor was it a mild fainting spell. Those could be brushed aside as pressure and nerves. This was a breakdown of epic proportions, the likes he had never seen before, and certainly not from the quick-witted Lauren who had so handily beaten him so often, whom he had never known to as much as flinch. Bottom line, watching Hill's mental deterioration and collapse wasn't the way he wanted to win a case. Yes, he needed to see justice served, and he believed it would be, but not at the expense of an esteemed peer. He was a competitor, but not that cold-blooded.

Seeing Judge Howell nodding her acknowledgment of Lauren's not-so-triumphant return to the stage actually relieved him. The reprimand would come at a later date and would likely not be too harsh.

Welcome back, Lauren, Dillon Bradley thought. And without further thought, he turned to his next witness, the gray-haired Beatrice Davis.

Back in charge and back in her comfort zone, Lauren was ready to resume. Real or not, she had come to terms with what she had seen and was determined to let it bother her no longer. Her only matter of concern was to push through this and win the case for her client. Then she could take a couple of days to relax and unwind. The last few weeks had been an emotional roller coaster for her. Speaking of her emotionally sensitive client, she hadn't given any thought to him since her return. She needed to establish how he had held up in her absence.

Lauren turned to face Maze. It didn't seem Maze had performed well on his own at all. He seemed worried, distraught, shaken up by her absence and the demons in his imaginative mind. Sweat was beading up on his forehead again. He looked like a pressure cooker seconds away from rupturing. Lauren leaned behind Ryan and gave Maze the stern, come-hither finger. Maze complied and leaned toward her.

"Why do you look worried?"

He didn't have a ready answer, but he was thinking, *Gee, I don't know, maybe it's because my attorney had a panic attack and ran out on me.* Not daring to voice what he felt, Maze simply shrugged.

"You look guilty," she whispered.

"I'm not."

"Listen, in love, war, and trials by jury, perception is everything." Lauren grit her teeth to let him know she was still the fiery-eyed tigress in charge of the lair. "Pull yourself together. Don't leave any room for doubt."

"Yeah, but is my attorney okay?"

Lauren tilted her head back, eyes ablaze. She wasn't inclined to say anything, just let him see her wrinkled brow and piercing eyes.

"If you're gonna bother worrying at all, worry about you and you alone." She sat up, crossing her arms over her chest. She tuned in to Bradley, who was finishing up a question.

"So, Mrs. Davis, you heard some shouting around eleven-twenty that evening?"

"Yes. I'm sure because I looked at my alarm clock."

"Shouting? A man and a woman?"

"Yes, a man and woman."

"And where was the shouting coming from, Mrs. Davis?"

"The adjoining cabin. Behind my head where I was trying to sleep."

"Okay, and what did you hear next?"

Mrs. Davis explained she had heard a terrible crash, the unmistakable shattering of glass, "like a huge window breaking." Maze sat fidgeting with his sealed medicine bottle as he listened to the woman's version of what happened. It didn't go unnoticed by the jurors.

Lauren was fully aware that the twelve were scrutinizing her client. Inside, she was boiling mad, but no one would know it by her exterior—pure cucumber. Although she couldn't seem to get it through Maze's thick skull that appearance wasn't just essential but everything, she had to keep her head. She reached over to get his attention. When he looked up, Lauren shot him a look for the ages.

"Mrs. Davis, the reason why I asked you back to the witness stand is to ask you this one question—to establish one thing that we feel wasn't established, before."

The witness nodded. Maze looked at Lauren and cowered, sending whispers amongst the jury.

Bradley continued. "Did you, at any time after hearing that initial *explosion*, hear any further shouting in the next cabin?"

"Heavens, no."

Gasps escaped from dismayed spectators. Bradley, content with his strategic move, had no further questions. Lauren, having nothing further to ask, declined cross-examination. Mrs. Davis was allowed to step down, and Osterman helped the old woman hobble back to her seat.

CHAPTER TEN

District Attorney Dillon Bradley was extremely pleased with how the day was progressing. Mrs. Davis' testimony was damning and unrefuted. The defendant Maze had lost his cool several times during the day, and Defense Attorney Hill had crumbled under pressure (but not so completely that he needed to feel bad about it). Granted, she had outsmarted him a time or two, but he had presented solid arguments for the twelve members of the jury to sink their teeth into, and he believed he had swayed them to his side. With only one witness remaining before the state rested its case, Bradley felt confident he was going to get a conviction and beat Lauren Hill. Sure, much of the evidence was circumstantial and some of the details a bit sketchy, but others had been convicted on less than what he and his team had presented.

Bradley was particularly happy to see that the witness now taking the stand had taken his advice and groomed himself better than he had the first time he had done so. Usually unkempt with long, greasy hair and covered from neck to toe with tattoos of skulls, snakes, and other satanic images, Larry Hendricks actually looked civilized. Granted, nothing short of laser surgery could remove his massive quantity of ink, but his hair was at least neatly trimmed, and he was cleanshaven.

Lauren, on the other hand, was angry, but she couldn't pinpoint exactly where that anger was directed. The trial had turned into a fiasco, and there was enough blame to go around. Maze obviously could have restrained himself better. However, given the circumstances, his behavior wasn't that much out of the ordinary for someone who, if found guilty, would be spending the rest of his life behind bars for murder one. No, Lauren had mostly herself to blame—even though her behavior was involuntary. Lauren could not for the life of her rationalize what she had seen within the scope of conventional science, but a meltdown was a meltdown, and that simply *CANNOT HAPPEN,* she admonished herself.

Now she was locked away inside herself, giving herself an internal pep talk to stay sane for just one more day. *Just one more day of stress,* she thought, *and then I'll be home free.* If she could only do for herself what Maze could not—keep herself in check and focus on the task at hand—she would be able to take that sabbatical away from the hustle and bustle of high-pressure lawyering, preferably someplace where the sand and tequila poured in equal, generous amounts.

A hand tapped hers, bringing her back to the present. Ryan gestured to her, then to Bradley, wanting her to object to his particular line of questioning. Lauren had been so distracted she hadn't heard any of what the opposition was discussing with the witness. She turned to listen.

"So the sliding glass door leading to the balcony was broken, shattered. But when you arrived, it had been mostly cleaned up. Who cleaned it?"

Lauren had to make a quick decision. She nodded to Ryan.

Ryan stood. "Objection. Assumes facts not in evidence."

"Overruled."

Hendricks waved an accusing finger at Maze. "He said he cleaned it."

"Let it be clear that Mr. Hendricks is pointing directly to the defendant, Maze." Bradley paused a moment. "So, then, where was all the glass?"

Lauren was back in the game. "Objection!"

"Overruled." Turning to the witness, Judge Howell instructed. "You may answer the question."

"I don't know. We didn't find none."

Exasperated, Bradley reworded the question. "If he cleaned it up, did the defendant explain where the broken glass was?"

"Oh, oh, yeah . . . overboard."

Lauren and Ryan both looked at Maze to clarify. Maze was already leaning toward his attorney. Adamantly, he said, "That's not how I said it."

Bradley, for dramatic effect, turned toward the defendant. "Overboard. He suspects his wife is missing and Mr. Maze is cleaning up broken shards of glass and throwing them overboard?" he said, mimicking a shoveling action.

Ryan's body language was practically screaming to object. Lauren, already foreseeing how it was going to play out, sat quietly going over her notes.

"Yeah, I guess so."

"Did he mention how the glass in the door broke?"

"His wife threw somethin' at it."

"Is that what Mr. Maze told you?"

"Yeah," Hendricks said.

"Did he say what she threw?"

"Nah."

Spectators began to murmur. Judge Howell banged the gavel twice, a friendly gesture reminding them where they were, as if any of them could have possibly forgotten.

"Thank you for your time, your patience, and your willingness to come back, Mr. Hendricks. Just one more question," Bradley paused. "When a passenger spills something or breaks one thing or another—let's say, for example, a towel rack or a mirror—do they usually clean it on their own or do they call housekeeping?"

Hendricks chuckled. "Nah. Don't remember no one cleanin' up for themselves."

"Perfect. Nothing further, Your Honor." Turning to Lauren, he added, "Your witness."

Lauren stood to cross-examine. She scanned the room, looking at all the combatants on the courtroom chessboard. All the knights and bishops were aligned to take the king, but they had forgotten where the opposing queen was positioned. Lauren sauntered toward the witness, but as she looked at Judge Howell—*Flash!*

God was sitting on the bench. Lauren slowed and did a double take. However, as quickly as He appeared, the Almighty vanished. Judge Howell rolled her eyes at Lauren, waiting impatiently for her to get on with it.

Spooked, but only for a moment, Lauren was determined not to let the vision interrupt her train of thought. She quickly regained her composure and coolly approached the witness box.

"How long were you the ship's housekeeping steward before the incident which brings us here today?"

Mr. Hendricks looked up at the ceiling, calculating. "June. October. 'Bout six months."

"Under six months?"

"About."

"My, my, my," she interrupted. "What if I told you I've added up the days? For the record, it was just over four months—four months and three days, to be precise."

"Yeah, sure. I guess."

Lauren glared at the witness. "I don't guess."

"Argumentative," Bradley called.

Although Lauren was nervous about even glancing toward the bench, she looked at Judge Howell. Mercifully, Howell was still human. The judge reminded Lauren that she hadn't asked a question.

"Move it along, counsel. Ask your questions, Ms. Hill."

Now displeased, Lauren looked up and glared at the judge, practically daring her to turn into God. She didn't. She glared back, motioning for her to speed up the process. Lauren shifted her position and checked her notes. Uncharacteristically, she had forgotten the question.

"Mr. State Witness—"

"Your Honor, argumentative."

Judge Howell began to speak. "Let her finish, Mr. Bradley."

Lauren turned to the judge, exasperated. Suddenly, a bright flash of light. God had usurped the bench, once more.

"Overruled," Lauren murmured, and walked to her table and poured herself a glass of water.

"What did you just say?" Judge Howell asked, unpleasantly.

Lauren wasn't expecting Judge Howell to be Judge Howell. She spun to face the bench. "What? Oh, nothing. Excuse me, Your Honor."

Judge Howell was not only not buying it, but also tiring of Lauren's insolence and was not going to take much more. She hadn't forgotten Lauren's earlier outbursts. She folded her arms and sat back as Lauren re-approached the witness stand.

"As I was saying, mine isn't a world of guessing, Mr. Hendricks, but one based upon facts in evidence. Now, let's examine under scrutiny your facts and bring them into evidence." She paused for dramatic effect, winked at Bradley, and turned back to the witness. Bradley leaned forward, interested.

"Where were you shortly before becoming the housekeeping manager of the cruise line?" Lauren asked.

Bradley and Osterman flew out of their respective chairs. In unison, they cried, "OBJECTION!"

"Sidebar, now!"

All three attorneys raced to the bench. Maze thought it the perfect opportunity to pester Ryan. He said he had heard from "reliable sources" that a jury finds a defendant guilty or not guilty the moment they see them.

Ryan turned with a bewildered look on his face. "Where did you hear that? That's not true."

Maze stared, studying Ryan. He was trying to decipher whether he believed what he was saying was true or handing him a line. "How do you know?"

"I'm a lawyer. That's how."

At the bench, another heated argument was underway. Neither side was willing to budge.

Osterman listened, wisely keeping his mouth shut to allow his boss the floor. Bradley was trying to keep his voice down, shouting in strained whispers. "This is so inappropriate. It has nothing to do with—"

Lauren jumped in. "Foundation, foundation, foundation."

"What foundation?" Judge Howell inquired.

"Establishing motive." Lauren was being purposefully vague.

"Motive?" Bradley shouted, unable to control himself. Incensed, he looked to Judge Howell for help. He saw he wasn't getting any from her. She seemed just as curious to see where Counsel Hill was going with her line of questioning. Still, she gave Lauren a strict warning not to cross any established lines.

Bradley threw his hands up. "I can't believe this," he said, starting for the table.

"Believe it, asshole," she said, following him away from the bench. Bradley turned to reply, but she was already walking away toward the witness stand.

"Mr. Prosecution Witness . . . "

"Objection. Argumentative. The witness has a name."

"Overruled."

"Mr. Well-Rehearsed."

Lauren glanced at her adversary who was bouncing his leg, obviously agitated. He scowled at her. Bradley wanted to object once more but wanted even more for her to get on with it.

"Do you need me to repeat the question for you?"

"Yeah, I guess," Hendricks replied.

"Where were you, let's say five months before the incident in question. Where did you call home?"

"Objection! The witness is not on trial, Your Honor."

"Overruled."

"Oh, c'mon! Like he said," and here Hendricks pointed to Bradley, "I'm not the one on trial, here."

"Just answer the question, Mr. Hendricks," she smirked.

Lawrence Hendricks puffed his cheeks out and released a large puff of air. "I was at Cal."

"Cal Tech? Cal State?"

"Not exactly." Hendricks fumed. Lowering his voice, he stated, "That's what we in the joint called Calipatria State Prison."

The jury collectively gasped.

Bradley knew it was futile. A jury cannot unhear what it has heard. However, he threw up his hands and gave a halfhearted "Objection."

Triumphantly, Lauren turned to Bradley. "Wow, prison—"

"Overruled."

"What were you incarcerated for, Mr. Hendricks?"

"Suspicion of selling."

Slipping the noose around his neck, she asked, "What, magazine subscriptions?"

The courtroom ruptured in laughter, prompting Judge Howell to bang her gavel. Lawrence Hendricks squirmed in his chair. His blood was boiling, but he somehow managed to keep a level head. Eventually, the room quieted.

"Drugs, okay. So what, I was in prison. Big deal."

"To me, and everyone here," Lauren gestured, "it is."

The witness was uncomfortable in his chair. She could see it. It was time to tighten the noose even further.

"Now, tell us, would you, how it was you happened to go from the Hotel Calipatria to such a coveted position as house keeping steward of the luxurious *Magical Quest?*"

Bradley didn't bother objecting. Lauren had eviscerated Hendricks already. Instead, he scratched his head, wondering how she had bested him on this one.

"My uncle is the purser."

"And so, do tell the court, is this your first cruise ship job?"

"Yeah, I guess."

"So, now, if I had to *guess*, like you seem to often do, I'd *guess* you had little to no housekeeping background, unless you count cleaning your cell after the guards had tossed it."

Bradley knew he should object to Lauren's badgering his witness, but by now even he was intrigued. He wanted to hear the next question as much as the judge and the jury, though he felt it would be painful to watch. Besides, what would a protest matter at that point? The quicker his witness was finished, the better.

"Therefore," Lauren continued, "you could not discern whether or not passengers were considerate, cleanly, slovenly, et cetera, yourself. Would that not be an accurate assessment of your lack of experience, Mr. Hendricks?"

Hendricks sat back in his chair, arms folded across his chest in front of him. A vein twitched at the top of his heated forehead as he scowled at the defense attorney.

"The witness will answer the question," Judge Howell reprimanded. "Be mindful you are still under oath."

"Thank you, Your Honor," said Lauren. "Look, I'm not trying to belittle you, Mr. Hendricks."

"You're sure doing a good job," Bradley muttered.

"In all likelihood, you do not know this, but as a defense attorney, this is my sixteenth murder trial. Now, would you say

I was experienced in murder trials?"

"Yeah, I guess so."

"And how many cruises had you been housekeeping manager on before the one in question, the one which Mr. Maze was on?"

Lawrence Hendricks took a deep breath. "Two," he said, irate.

"Two? Okay, fine. Now, using my sixteen trials as a measure, would you say that you are experienced in cruise ship passenger habits, based on only two cruises before the one Mr. Maze was on?"

Hendricks pondered a moment. "Yeah. I mean, no. Sure, I guess I'm not that experienced."

"Well, given only two, of course you aren't. But now, shifting gears: as to the broken glass, are you completely sure my client told you he threw it overboard?"

"I don't know where else it could have gone. He said he cleaned it up! Fine. I don't 'zactly 'member what he said he did with the glass."

Bradley sat back in his chair, fuming. It would have been nice to know that tidbit before Hendricks' taking the stand. He'd just made everyone on the prosecution look extremely bad.

"Well thank you, Mr. Hendricks, for your candid participation in getting to the truth, today. Your Honor, we are done here." Lauren faced Bradley and smacked her notes against her open palm. *Touché!*

Although he hated closing on a sour note, Bradley had no other option. Hendricks had been his last witness. "Your Honor, the state rests," he said, dejectedly.

Given the hour of the day, Judge Howell made a few general statements to the jury, and that was it. Court was then adjourned until the following morning.

The judge felt as if she had been through a war zone. Frankly, she was glad the case was finally coming to an end. She requested that both lead counsels join her in her chambers directly afterward to discuss, among other things, closing arguments.

CHAPTER ELEVEN

J ustice Susan Howell gracefully slipped off her robe and hung it on the freestanding coatrack in the far corner. Although two metal hooks had been mounted on the wall near the entrance specifically for that purpose, she never used them. She was a woman of superstition and habit, much more comfortable with the old. In fact, besides the wooden coatrack, several other antiquated items graced the newly remodeled office. She could not bring herself to part with the mantle clock which she had to painstakingly wind every three days or so, her father's Remington Noiseless typewriter from the 1920s, or an old fan whose three blades reminded her of old aircraft propellers. Although it no longer oscillated properly, the relic always hummed to life when she threw the switch. *They sure don't make 'em like that anymore,* she often thought.

Judge Howell told her law clerk to take the rest of the day off, as she would be discussing court matters with the two opposing counsels regarding the Maze case. The young clerk didn't have to be told twice. Excitedly, she organized her things, grabbed her purse, and rushed out to bask in the Southern California sun. With light traffic that time of day, she figured she would be relaxing at Venice Beach in just over an hour.

Grabbing a Diet Coke from the personal refrigerator next to her desk—one of the few modern amenities she found useful and necessary—the judge went to the picture frame on the wall behind her desk. Every day she looked at this handwritten letter from John Quincy Adams to her great-great-grandfather on her mother's side, congratulating him on becoming a Supreme Court justice. Her mother had handed it down to her the day Howell had been sworn in. Twelve years had passed since then. Howell admired the smooth, flowing strokes of the president's quill. She couldn't imagine what it must have been like having to write such lengthy documents with a feather.

Judge Howell pulled the top on her can of soda. As the seal broke, she heard the familiar hiss of released carbonation. A rush of tiny droplets rose into the air, and she breathed in the sweetness of aspartame. She realized it wasn't good for human consumption, but she couldn't have the real stuff. It would send her sugar levels through the roof. Besides, she believed she was entitled to a vice or two. She took a long sip.

As she was about to sit down and go through the messages of the day, the anticipated knock came. Through the door, Judge Howell could hear the familiar voices of the bailiff yukking it up with District Attorney Dillon Bradley. Above the loudness of their voices, she told them to enter.

The voices grew quiet as the bailiff opened the door. Lauren Hill stepped inside, followed immediately by Bradley. As it was a private meeting, the bailiff closed the door behind him as he left.

Judge Howell quickly began flipping through her messages. Bradley went to sit down, but without looking up, the judge said, "No, please. This will only take a moment." Lauren, seizing the opportunity, whipped out her cell phone. Deftly, she thumbed her reply to the inquiry made earlier. Like the question—*Sex?*—her answer was a simple, three-letter response—*Yes*. She quickly tucked her phone into a pocket inside her purse and spun around to face Judge Howell.

Taking a mental inventory, Susan Howell set the rest of her messages aside and addressed both attorneys.

"So, the state has rested," she said, glancing at her watch. "I realize it's just after one-thirty, but I prefer to start fresh tomorrow morning. And Ms. Hill, are you planning to put your client on the stand?"

Lauren was a bit startled, though. She thought it was much later. Checking her watch, she confirmed the time was only 1:36. Today must have *really* rattled her, if she wasn't even able to keep track of the time.

"No, your Honor."

Bzzzzz. Bradley's phone vibrated inside his jacket pocket. He casually reached for it.

Looking directly at Lauren, Judge Howell scolded. "And what the hell were you doing, earlier? It's so unlike you, Counselor."

Lauren looked down toward the floor.

"Your conduct was—"

Lauren's shoulders slumped.

Reading the text, Bradley chuckled. "I believe it's generally called cracking under pressure."

It was the distraction Lauren was hoping for. "Piss off, Bradley. Cracked, my ass. Exactly how many cases against me have you won?" Lauren placed the tip of her index finger against her thumb and held up the symbol to him. "Zero!"

Bradley felt that like a spear thrust in his side. It hurt, and she had meant it to hurt.

"But who's counting the near misses, right?" she added, twisting the knife.

Bzzz! Judge Howell's phone sounded.

"Excuse me," she said. "Let me get rid of this."

With Judge Howell momentarily distracted, Bradley whispered, "But you still said I was the best sex you ever had."

Laura smugly replied softly, "May I remind you that was ten years ago. Since then, you've taken a nosedive. You've fallen way off the charts."

Having finished with her call, Judge Howell cut in. "Whoa—whoa! We're crash landing headfirst into mistrial land!"

Judge Howell shook her head and took a deep, cleansing breath. Playing it cool, she continued.

"Well, the inordinate hostility between you two makes a little more sense, now. Nevertheless, Mr. Bradley, just to confirm, are the people prepared to start closing tomorrow morning?"

"Yes, Your Honor."

"Good. Timewise, I'll give each of you three hours, Mr. Prosecutor, an additional hour for rebuttal."

"Could I get an hour and a half?"

"Blowhard!" Lauren interjected.

Looking at Lauren sternly, Judge Howell concurred. Although she believed the added half hour was fair, the judge didn't care one way or the other. As long as it went off without a hitch, unlike the present day no one was enjoying. "Any other objections?"

"No, Your Honor. That's fine." Bradley said.

"Kiss-ass." Lauren puckered her lips for emphasis.

Seeing her with those guppy lips, Bradley chuckled. "And that's just the foreplay."

"It's a turn-off."

"Okay, you two. Ms. Hill, are we in agreement?"

Lauren reluctantly nodded.

"All right, then, I'll see each of you tomorrow." Then, as an afterthought, she added, "Oh, and let's keep the bitter memories to a minimum, shall we?" Without another word, Judge Howell turned, grabbed her portfolio and appointment book, and went directly to work.

Taking the cue, Lauren and Dillon made their way toward the exit. Dillon opened the door for Lauren, but she would have none of the sexist attitude and motioned for him to exit ahead of her. She could get her own door, thank you very much. Shrugging his shoulders in a suit-yourself motion, he did.

"Lauren."

The soft-spoken, all-too-familiar voice behind her caused Lauren to stop in her tracks. It wasn't the stern yet sometimes pleasant, feminine voice she was accustomed to hearing in that office and had taken direction from over the past several days. No, the voice calling to her was decidedly masculine: a voice of reason, commanding attention without being demanding. She had heard it before, been lectured by it, even, at inconvenient intervals throughout the day. One thing about it was painfully clear—Lauren Hill never wanted to hear that voice again.

The voice wasn't frightening, but it frightened her. Lauren was comfortable being in charge of her own life. She didn't want to be held accountable for her actions. She wanted to do what she wanted to do, when and how she wanted to do it: a rogue wolf in sheep's clothing. That's what she intended upon doing. Only, there was just one Being preventing her from doing so. With God, there was no way she could get away with her plans. Without being convicting, the voice convicted her.

Lauren gazed down the hallway to see if Dillon had heard the voice as well. It was obvious to her he hadn't. At least he didn't acknowledge he had. He just kept walking briskly straight ahead, whistling. She watched as he disappeared around the corner. Lauren thought to call to him, but she didn't want him thinking her crazy if it only turned out to be her imagination run amok.

Silence behind her. Not so much as the rustling of paper. Maybe she had imagined it. Then she realized something was missing. The part of herself that always listened for ticking clocks alerted her that it shouldn't be this quiet. The distinctive droning of the pendulum inside Judge Howell's mantle clock had ceased.

This can't possibly be good, she thought.

"Lauren."

She turned. "Judge Howell?" Lauren placed a dainty hand upon her forehead and applied pressure. "If you're God, and I'm not going crazy, why are you talking to me?"

She began to cry uncontrollably. *I'm going insane. It's happening. I can feel it. It's happening. It's happening. No—no— NO!*

God approached Lauren. But the closer He got to her, the further to the floor she slid.

"Noooo, noooo," she whimpered.

God looked down upon the crumpled form of Lauren Hill. Pitying her, He bent to cradle her in His arms. In them, she found comfort. His noble features and calming reassurance soothed and quieted her. Lauren's tears dried as she looked into the deep wells of His eyes.

"You are not insane, Lauren."

"Then what am I?"

"I suppose some would use the word 'blessed.' But I would say 'forewarned.'"

Suddenly, Lauren was looking, not at God, but at Judge Howell cradling her and trying to assess what was wrong with her. Startled, Lauren twitched.

"I'm calling a doctor," said Judge Howell.

"What, what for?" Lauren asked, coming to her senses.

"You passed out."

"I did?—No, no, no, no, I didn't!"

"You most certainly did," she paused. "Less you're having some sort of nervous breakdown."

Lauren shook her off and scrambled to her feet. "No! No! You're right. I just passed out. Low blood sugar," she said, reaching for her purse. "Stress!"

"I think you need to see a doctor."

Lauren wiped her tear-drenched eyes. "No, please. No, thank you, completely fine. Have a candy bar in my purse. Should've eaten lunch." Lauren tore open the wrapper of a Pay Day and began ravenously devouring it. Peanut halves fell to the floor. "Just a little hungry, that's all. I'll be fine, now."

Judge Howell stood shaking her head. She wasn't buying it, but Lauren was already moving toward the door.

"See you tomorrow. Gotta run. Closing arguments." Lauren dashed out of the judge's chambers. "Closing arguments!"

As if warding off evil, Judge Howell shut the door. She sat behind her desk, pulled a flask from the bottom drawer, and poured it into the can of Diet Coke. She sat back, glad the day was over.

"Some days, there just isn't enough alcohol."

CHAPTER TWELVE

Lauren met up with Ryan and Maze in the main corridor by the front entrance of the courthouse. Ryan was gazing intently out one of the windows to the street below. Maze spotted Lauren coming down the crowded hallway. How could he not? He had the hottest-looking attorney in the county. He tapped Ryan on the shoulder and pointed in her direction.

Ryan waited until his boss was close to inform her that the press hounds had gathered at the base of the steps. Lauren glanced out the window. There they were, not so patiently waiting to conduct interviews with the principal players.

"So they are. We knew this, though. Let them have their day in the California sun."

Lauren turned to Maze and shook her head. He was an untidy mess. Motherly instincts took over. She immediately went to work sprucing him up. She straightened his tie and jacket while telling him to run a comb through his matted hair. While Lauren groomed Maze, she prepared him as best she could to face the media. Plucking a tiny, practically unnoticeable lint ball off the front of his jacket, Lauren held it up.

"Cameras catch every flaw, and that includes character flaws," she said. "Look sharp. Be sharp. Got it?"

Although he had never quite been able to get used to how demanding Lauren was, Maze did as instructed. He wasn't stupid; he understood everything she said. He wasn't willful or naturally rebellious. He was just scared out of his mind and sometimes had difficulty focusing.

"You still look guilty, though," Ryan said unkindly.

Maze cringed. Lauren shot Ryan a "must you?" look.

What? I was only kidding."

As confident as she could be in her client's appearance, Lauren led her team down the courthouse steps to the gauntlet below. "Just act natural."

Easy for her to say, Maze thought. *This could very well be my last night of freedom.*

As the trio reached the last tier of steps, camera shutters opened and bulbs started flashing. Anxious reporters converged, thrusting microphones before them.

"Ms. Hill, Ms. Hill."

Holding a hand up, Lauren informed them that, one at a time, she would take their questions.

The first question, which she knew was coming, was what had happened to her earlier to make her exit the courtroom so abruptly. Not caring if anyone bought into her explanation, she told them she had a migraine so debilitating it had affected her vision. Stress sometimes brought them on, but until that moment, never in a courtroom situation. She had simply panicked.

"Oh, come on, Ms. Hill," one reporter provoked. "I saw how you ran out of there. Looked as if something scared you pretty bad."

"And it wasn't the judge," another chimed in.

Nervous laughter.

Lauren refused to comment and deflected all questions. Like it or not, that was her recollection of the incident. That was all she was going to say about it. Nothing further was asked. The media saw she wasn't about to reveal anything different.

"Maze—Maze! This is for Maze. Outbursts today. Can you elaborate on them? Do you have faith in your attorney?"

Maze was noticeably camera-shy but leaned toward the microphones to speak. Lauren jumped in to save him from embarrassment.

"It isn't easy for a blameless man to remain silent in the face of wrongful persecution."

"Then why doesn't he just testify?" a TV 6 reporter said, shoving a handheld tape recorder in her face.

Maze leaned in. "I want—"

Lauren cut him off. "It's not incumbent on Mr. Maze to defend his innocence, but for the prosecution to prove his guilt. We'll take one more question."

"Ms. Hill, are you worried at all that the state has made a compelling case?"

Lauren laughed. "Firing spitballs at a fortified battleship, that's all they're actually doing, firing spitballs at a battleship. They have nothing."

The three of them started walking away as Prosecutor Bradley and his team descended the steps for their turn at the microphones. Bradley looked at them with a twinkle in his eye. Lauren kept walking with hardly a glance upward.

"Hey, what did Judge Howell say?" Ryan inquired.

Lauren knew her assistant was fishing for information about any repercussions for her earlier erratic behavior, but she told him only that she and Bradley were given three hours each for closing arguments and the prosecution an hour and a half for rebuttal.

"I'm having nightmares again," Maze blurted out.

"Then don't sleep," Lauren said, sharply, as she turned to listen to Bradley's conference.

"Mr. Bradley, do you know what was happening with the

defense today, the strange behavior?" a reporter asked.

Osterman and a few reporters chuckled. Bradley turned to his young attorney, giving him a disapproving look. Then, turning back to the microphones, he said, "Strange? In what way?" Without waiting for a reply, he continued. "Look, we're all under a great deal of pressure here. To be honest, no, I didn't notice anything too much out of the ordinary."

Ryan, turning to Maze, showed a burst of compassion. "I'll see if I can't get you something over the counter."

Rolling her eyes, Lauren leaned toward Ryan. "We should have requested a ball gag order."

"You mean just a gag ord—"

"I mean," she interrupted, "A good penis checker." Lauren made a hard, chopping motion in the air.

In spite of the enormous pressure, Ryan and Maze laughed. It was exactly what was needed to break the thick ice. Both men seemed to relax more.

Bradley flagged another question, and Lauren perked up.

"What makes you so sure Maze murdered his wife and that she didn't take her own life?"

"This, coming from a woman who's appeared on *Nancy Grace* three times," Ryan said disapprovingly.

"Four," Lauren corrected. "Oh, I wish the windbag would just shut up for once."

"I believe the evidence speaks loud and clear for itself," Bradley answered. "Some things are just obvious."

Lauren checked her watch.

Maze, head down, caught her attention as he started to ramble. "But it's hard, you know, harder than it was before. I find myself living that night, again and again, only it's different in my memory. It's dark, very, very dark. These focused freeze-frames, so vivid, in sharp detail, detail that you could never see with the naked eye. Each word we said to one another echoes as they didn't, then. And the regrets, the regrets, so minor, but so deep." He raised his head and continued. "Then I come here, day after day; I listen to them try to paint the picture, the picture that didn't exist, and connect dots that were never there. I feel guilty, even if I'm not, I still feel guilty."

"Hey, Maze," Ryan offered. "It's just how the prosecution framed their argument. We've shown that not only do the dots not connect, they never existed in the first place."

"I know you've done your best, but I can't help wondering 'what if.'"

"There are no 'what ifs,'" Lauren replied.

"No, 'what ifs?' Well, what if it is a hung jury? I have to relive it all, again."

Lauren looked directly into Maze's weepy eyes. "Listen to me. If you are not guilty—and you are not guilty—then you win. No compunction. No shame. Win." Lauren checked her watch and looked up at Bradley.

He was answering another question. "This is obviously a court of law. It's not about winning or even punishment. It's about justice being served."

"Look, I've gotta run. Preparing for closing arguments, tomorrow." Lauren leaned into Ryan. "Keep an eye on our boy for me."

CHAPTER THIRTEEN

L auren was weaving her way through downtown Los
Angeles traffic. She was preoccupied and narrowly escaped
accident and injury, twice. Each would have been her fault,
so to save face, she slammed on the horn and screamed through
air-conditioned space at the opposing driver.

How could she not be distracted? The visions, if that was what
she could call them, replayed over and over again in her mind.
It was dangerous for her to be behind the wheel in this state,
but no one was allowed to drive her vehicle, not her colleagues
and certainly not her useless husband. Let him drive the wagon.
Besides, where she was going, he could never be allowed to find
out. No one could. It would mean more than just her career, but
never practicing law again. However, she wasn't the least bit
nervous. When it came to infidelity, just as in the courtroom,
Lauren was clever.

Her mind a distant elsewhere, Lauren ran a red light. She
came to a screeching halt just inches from a six-figure Maserati.
That would have made the old insurance premiums skyrocket.
Fortunately for her, the Maserati's owner only yelled a few choice

obscenities before speeding up the ramp to the 405 Freeway. It was unlike her to be so inattentive, and she had just been behind the wheel fifteen minutes.

Get your shit together, woman! Lauren scolded herself.

Today was decidedly the weirdest, most disconcerting day in court she had ever had. Lauren had always prided herself on being nothing less than on her A-game at all times. What had happened today? It had started like any other, but then quickly soured once she arrived at court. Running out of the courtroom in near hysterics wasn't the last image she had planned on leaving with the impressionable jury.

At least there were a few shining moments to be proud of, especially how she'd manipulated Bradley's last witness. *What possessed Dillon to use that creep?* she wondered. Not only that, there was the consolation of closing arguments that would hopefully set everything to rights, provided she could get enough sleep to prevent a second mental breakdown.

True, God had tried to assure her she was not going insane, but when your hallucination is the one telling you that you aren't crazy, maybe you are. She felt she was teetering on a precipice, dangerously close to toppling over into spending the rest of her days at some group home with bars on the windows for the mentally disturbed. Nor did she now believe that the personage conveniently popping in and out of her life during a good portion of the day was, in fact, The Almighty. The subconscious mind could play awful tricks on a person.

Lauren whipped her smoky gray Lexus into the hotel parking lot and jumped out. As fast as her flashy high heels would allow, she sprinted to the door and paid for the room. She was in control and had no intention of giving him the satisfaction of paying. The attendant handed her the keycard and Lauren walked briskly to the elevator, texting as she went without ever missing a beat.

Lauren slid the key into the slot, opened the door, and kicked her shoes off. She was rubbing her tired feet when the door flung open.

"Spitballs? Battleships?" Bradley muttered.

"Thought you'd never get here. Did your mother have to drive you?"

"Stuck in traffic."

Looking lustfully upon her, he wasted no time. Hastily, he unbuttoned her blouse.

"I just love these," he whispered hungrily as he dove between her breasts. He reached up with both hands, cupping them roughly thru the lacy material.

Lauren moaned, brutally running her manicured fingers thru his windblown hair. Bradley led her to the bed and fell on top of her.

Everything was a game to Lauren. In this one, she was just as ravenous as he, but today she couldn't concentrate. Damn those visions!

Sensing her distraction, Bradley sat up. "What's wrong?"

Lauren looked up at him with a blank expression.

"What is it? Did I do something?"

Bradley saw a tear welling in the corner of her eye. She closed her eyes. It ran down her cheek. Bradley had never seen her in such a distressed state. In that moment, even though they were fulfilling their carnal desires, he had a deep affinity, if not a fondness, for her that transcended the mere physical.

She shook her head. "No."

"Lauren?" he whispered.

"Don't call me that."

"You call me Dillon. If not your name, what should I call you?"

"Just don't say my name, not like that."

Bradley backed away, hands up in a no-harm, no-foul gesture. Lauren shifted her position and, grabbing a tissue off the nightstand, wiped the moisture from her eyes. She was beside herself and yet comfortable enough in the presence of someone who honestly couldn't hold it against her. She turned to him.

"I'm scared," Lauren confessed.

Bradley's eyes widened in surprise.

"Yeah, I'm scared, okay? Scared that lunacy is finally catching up with me."

The revelation had Bradley at a loss for words. "What?"

"It's in my blood, my fucked-up, fucking blood. Uhhgh!" Lauren paused, then laughed nervously. "My mother. My fucking mother went insane. Yeah, when I was about in second grade. Yeah, around that time. Now I'm afraid it's happening to me, too. She was thirty-four. I guess it took a little longer to catch up with me."

Dillon had no idea how to respond or how to act for that matter. Hell, he didn't even know what Lauren was trying to convey. However, he was committed to giving her the space she needed.

In spite of her rapidly deteriorating emotional state, Lauren reached behind her and unhooked her bra, in defiance of the demons closing in on her. Bradley couldn't help but be aroused by her sculpted form. Lauren took off her blouse and turned to him.

"You know, it's funny," she mused. "My grandfather had her committed. He was pretty much a dyed-in-the-wool rat bastard. But under the circumstances, I don't know what else he could have done. She damn near burned the house down because she said the Virgin Mary told her to."

This tidbit left Bradley no longer sexually excited. However, he was mesmerized by her uncharacteristic vulnerability. "Where was your father when all this was going on?"

"I never knew my father," Lauren replied a little distantly. Then she shook herself slightly and turned back to him. "We gonna fuck now or not?"

He managed a come-hither grin and Lauren pushed him flat on his back and hungrily began unbuckling his belt. She straddled him, and he halfheartedly reached for her breasts. He tried not to think about Lauren's disturbing revelation, but he was not going to be able to perform his manly function no matter how gorgeous the woman pawing at his pants was.

Suddenly, she jumped off him. "Think they have a Bible here?"

Dillon was even more confused but also secretly glad he wouldn't have to come up with a lame excuse as to why he couldn't sustain an erection. Lauren stumbled to the dresser and Dillon began flinging the drawers open. In the third one, she saw the Gideon. Bradley sat up, watching her in strained amusement as she frantically thumbed through the pages.

"You're Catholic, right?" she asked.

Dillon nodded.

"Where's Proverbs?"

"Ah, somewhere in the middle, I think."

"Gotta find 6:16."

Lauren increased her speed, tearing several pages in the process. Finally, she stopped and turned a couple more pages, slowly. She paused and began to read aloud.

"These six things doth the Lord hate, yea, seven are an abomination to him: A proud look, a lying tongue, and hands that shed innocent blood, a heart that deviseth wicked imaginations, feet that be swift in running to mischief, a false witness that speaketh lies, and he that soweth discourse among brethren. My son, keep thy father's commandment, and forsake not the law of thy mother: bind them continually upon thine heart, and tie them about thy neck. When thou goest, it shall lead thee; when thou sleepest, it shall keep thee; and when thou awakest, it shall talk with thee, for the commandment is a lamp, and the law is light, and reproofs of instruction are the way of life." She turned to Dillon and abruptly asked, "Do you think God hates us?"

"Uh . . . " he wasn't ready to play Twenty Questions. "Why? Because of a serious breach of ethics?"

"No, damn it. Because of this," she waved her hand. "What

we're doing. It's unproductive, nothing but pure lust!"

Bradley had no idea how to respond. He came anticipating a hotel rendezvous with a professional adversary. He may not win the court case, but he wanted to go home a winner at something. But this seemed to be slipping from his grasp too. He was exasperated and sexually frustrated but somehow felt as exhausted as if he had sex.

Lauren was tired. Her head was spinning a mile a minute. For the third time in one day, she felt her headache returning with a vengeance. Nonchalantly, she tossed the Good Book back into the drawer and closed each drawer carefully. She brushed her hair with her fingers and quickly buttoned her blouse. In more ways than one, she felt naked, exposed, and somehow dirty.

"I don't know if you saw anything, today, but I had some kind of—"

Lauren checked her words. She couldn't reveal everything, not just yet. She still had a career to think about.

"I had some kind of anxiety attack, today. In fact, several." Lauren beat her open palm against her forehead. "But why? Why? I've never had one before, and I get three in rapid succession. What if I'm going—"

Bat-shit crazy, she wanted to say.

"Fuck, fuck, fuck!" She paused. "I don't know, but I swear it was like . . . oh gawd, my head hurts."

Bradley had heard enough. He had let Lauren vent and get it all out. But he wasn't about to allow her to beat herself up believing she was going insane. She was too good a lawyer, too good a professional, too good an acquaintance for that to be taking place. It was simply one off day in a series of extremely stressful days during a high-pressure case. And even at her worst, Lauren had performed brilliantly.

"Whoa, Lauren. I refuse to believe you're going insane. I don't believe for one minute. Hey, you know something, for someone who had a self-admitted anxiety attack, you sure took it to us, this morning."

"You're being far too kind."

"No, not really."

"I mean to yourself. I kicked your ass today."

Dillon snickered. In spite of everything, she had.

Lauren's cell rang. She grabbed her purse and plunged into it to retrieve the phone. Looking at the caller ID, she rolled her eyes.

"What?"

Lauren's husband was in a tight situation. Normally, he wouldn't have attempted to reach her during business hours, given she was in the middle of a trial. He knew how she felt about that. However, he had called Lauren's secretary to leave a message, and finding out court had adjourned early to start fresh the next morning with closing arguments, he decided to call her direct.

"Court is in recess for the rest of the day, why?"

"So where are you, now?" her husband, Dennis, asked.

"Having a late lunch with an associate."

"Can you cut it short and pick Constance up from practice?"

"Just because I'm out of court early doesn't . . . Why can't you get her?"

"I've got a meeting with the publisher. Sounds promising."

"It did the last two times, too. Never mind. Yeah, I'll get her." Lauren looked at her watch. "Call her and tell her I'll be a few minutes late, but to wait for me."

CHAPTER FOURTEEN

Constance Hill was much like any other 21ˢᵗ-century American girl: a bouncy, frivolous adolescent with a flippant, devil-may-care attitude. Like most high school freshmen, she was vibrant, full of youth and vitality, although she could be on the lazy side when it came to doing things that didn't suit her. Intelligent to the point of knowing just about everything—or at least thinking she did—she tended to voice her opinion, especially when it came to the adult female in her household. For Lauren, the girl always had a mouth. Mother and daughter butted heads like two alpha rams.

Constance was fourteen going on forty. Because her mother worked long hours and her dad was usually behind the locked door of his study staring at a blank computer screen and suffering from writer's block, the impressionable adolescent was not well supervised. She wore too much makeup, skirts too short, and bras too padded for either of her parents' liking. The only thing that remained from her early childhood was the way she wore her hair—ponytail, always a ponytail.

With squealing tires, her mother raced around the corner into the Jefferson High School parking lot, going twice as fast as the twenty-mile-per-hour posted speed limit. Constance, watching her mother's approach, popped a bubble with the two pieces of grape bubblegum she had crammed into her mouth and rolled her eyes. *Not her. Not today,* she thought.

Lauren forcefully applied the brakes and came to a bone-jarring halt in front of the school, tapping the front bumper of another parent's vehicle. She mouthed *Sorry* at the other driver. "Idiot," she said as Constance flung the back door open and craned her neck to look inside.

"*You're* picking me up? Seriously?"

"Yeah, c'mon, get in. Sit up front."

Constance closed the back door and repeated the process with the front door. "Why? Where's Dad? Is he hurt?"

If I could only be so lucky, Lauren thought. "Glad to see you, too. And no, he's not hurt, sick, or dying. Seems your father has a meeting with his publisher or something."

Constance wasn't sure she wanted a ride from her mother after all and briefly contemplated walking the three and a half miles home.

"C'mon, get in, already. I haven't got all day. I have to prepare for closing arguments in the morning."

"Oh, alright," Constance said, exasperated.

Not understanding, or, better yet, not particularly giving a damn about pick-up and drop-off procedures, Lauren gunned it as another parent pulled in front of her. Lauren swerved and jammed the brake, narrowly missing the other vehicle. A girl in the back seat was frantically waving to get Constance's attention. She smiled and waved back.

Lauren blasted the horn.

"What the hell is wrong with these morons? Where the hell did she get her license, a Cracker Jack box?"

"Mom! Oh, my gawd! That's Jessica's mom."

"I don't give a flaming rat's ass whose mom it is. We're not pitting at the Indy 500, here. Get your seatbelt on."

"Already did."

"C'mon, move it, already," Lauren shouted, blaring the car horn.

Constance slid lower in her seat, as far as her seatbelt would allow, and covered her face out of sheer embarrassment. Hastily, Jessica's mother pulled ahead to let the mentally deranged woman behind her maneuver. She watched as Lauren sped away, missing her Chevy Caprice by mere inches.

"See, this is what happens when you have nothing to do all day but go from Home Depot to the grocery store to get cupcakes and garden shears."

"Really, Mom? Cupcakes and garden shears?"

"Yeah, I'd like to see them work in the real world."

"And what world do they live in, mom?"

"Like the one your father lives in, Make-Believe Land. Where you get to sit home on your ass and confuse creativity with productivity."

Lauren turned to Constance in time to see the blank expression on her daughter's face.

"Oh, whatever," Lauren said, and then added after a pause, "anyway, how was your day?"

"Really, Mom? What do you care?"

"Don't give me that attitude, young lady! If I didn't care, I wouldn't have bothered asking."

Constance wasn't convinced, yet she truly wanted to tell her some exciting news, exciting to her, anyway. She had been chosen by her peers to be the junior varsity captain of the basketball team. Constance took a deep breath and began to dive in.

"Constance," her mother interrupted, "I want you to know something."

Constance sat back, arms folded across her chest.

"I'm not going to go insane on you. Promise."

Constance so wanted to say something sarcastic based on her behavior back at school, such as *"You could have fooled me,"* but wisely decided not to press her luck. She didn't want to get grounded so close to the weekend. She was invited to a party, and it would be tragic not to be able to go. Everyone who was anyone was going to be there.

Insane? Where did that come from, anyway?

"What, you have nothing to say to that?" Lauren pressed.

Constance let her mother have it. "What?" she said sarcastically, "Like you're gonna miraculously turn into a real mother, all of a sudden?"

Lauren was incensed. "What the hell is that supposed to mean? Nah, I know exactly what it means. You and your father have a little cabal against me. A conspiracy. That's what this is, and I'm *always* the bad guy."

Constance thought about changing the subject, but the damage had already been done. Normally, the girl thrived on being argumentative with her mom, but practice had been particularly grueling that afternoon. She was exhausted, and she suddenly had the urge to go to the bathroom. Raising her voice was putting undue pressure on her full bladder.

"Please, can we just get home?"

Lauren hadn't exactly had an easy day either, so she was just about to table the argument when her eye caught some doodling on her daughter's notebook. Alternating glances between the road and the notebook several times, she deciphered some rather unfavorable writing. It read *Love Dad* with a heart and a smiley face next to it. Underneath, in bold letters, she clearly read, *Hate Mom.* Lauren's hurt turned into anger. She was furious, but the lawyer with nerves of steel managed to remain relatively calm.

"So, you want to change the subject. Okay, wanna tell me what that says in your notebook?"

Oh, no! Constance thought. *Mom sees everything.* Constance quickly covered the wording with her open palm. "Nothing," she muttered.

"Move your hand!"

"Mom, it's nothing . . . nothing! It's just about boys!"

Exasperated, Lauren whipped a sharp turn. Tires squealing, the car lurched forward and jolted to an abrupt stop. She was certainly giving the suspension a workout. Lauren turned the engine off and faced her willful daughter.

"Lying to me? Move your hand; don't you lie to me, missy!" Lauren yanked her daughter's hand away and read, *Love Dad. Hate Mom.*

Busted! Constance was bathed in guilt. Blushing, she lowered her head in shame, no longer wanting to spew smart-alecky phrases. She was caught red-handed in a hurtful lie. Nothing to explain. Nothing she said could make a difference. Those malicious words were plainly in front of her, boldly written in blue ink for teachers and friends alike to read.

Of course, for Constance to have written such spiteful words, she had to be hurting. But Lauren could not see beyond her own grief as a parent. In her anger, she didn't take the time to work out the *whys* behind her daughter's negative feelings. This kind of attitude was inexcusable. Lauren worked long hours to provide for her ungrateful daughter's needs. Constance was all smiles when she needed clothes or a new iPad. Then, Mom was good enough. All those niceties came with a price that Lauren had to pay—long, sometimes tedious hours slumped over thick texts or talking to people she didn't even like.

It was Lauren—not Dennis—who had supplied most of her child's physical needs, and Lauren couldn't understand why he got all of Constance's love and affection. She couldn't see that Constance didn't just want the material things. Constance didn't have the motherly support most other girls her age had, and she missed it. Lauren was too wrapped up in her own selfish desires to see the damage those long hours away inflicted on their relationship. She could see that there was a wedge driven between them, but she refused to see that she herself may have been the cause of such animosity. Although Constance was fourteen and gaining more independence, she still needed and longed for a closer bond with her mother.

Instead of trying to both logically and lovingly get to the crux of the situation by speaking in civil tones and getting to the real reasons behind the feelings, Lauren became incensed.

"Is that true?" she growled. "Is this how you feel?"

Constance tried to look away as a tear escaped. She didn't loathe her mother. Those words had been written out of hurt and frustration, as her mother missed basketball games, rehearsals, and more importantly, mother-daughter talks. All her friends had mothers who did all those things. They reveled in their children's accomplishments and comforted them in their failures. It would never have occurred to them to miss out on them. Constance didn't have that, and she felt it missing from her life.

"Look at me!" Lauren demanded, her voice rising. "Well, that's real nice. I seem to recall taking the time to push you out of my body, and don't think it was easy."

Any feeling of remorse for what she had done was now replaced with defiance as Constance rolled her eyes. *Here it comes. That same tired, worn-out "I gave birth to you" line. Isn't childbirth natural?*

If Lauren didn't want a child, why did she have one? Constance didn't ask to be brought into the world, and since she was here, her mother had the moral obligation to not only take care of and nurture her but to take the time to be interested and invested in her life. It didn't seem too much to ask to spend a few hours a week with her.

It was no use. She wasn't making any headway. Her mother was wrapped up in herself. Constance did what all teenagers do; she tuned her out.

"Twenty-three hours' worth of not easy," Lauren was shouting now. "I really don't know why you insisted on staying in there, anyway. But do you honestly understand what it is I do all day?" It was a rhetorical question: Lauren was on a roll. "There's one powerful group of people using every trick in the book to take powerless people's lives away. And I, I stand in the way of them just doing what they want to do. That requires a great deal of time, concentration, and commitment. Do you understand me?"

"Yeah, but what do you get for it?" Constance retorted.

"I get compensated very well so that I'm able to provide us with a roof over our heads and clothes on our backs."

Dead silence for a long moment as Lauren took a deep breath and Constance stared into the distance.

Lauren saw the faraway expression on her daughter's face. "Why do you hate me so?"

"I don't," Constance answered.

"It says so, right there." Lauren tapped on the notebook.

In true lawyer's daughter's fashion, Constance replied, "I could ask you the same thing."

Stunned, Lauren paused. She lowered her voice. "Honey, I don't hate you. I never said that."

She leaned over to hug her daughter. But Constance turned away; her mother's actions of late spoke louder than words, and Constance wanted a real commitment, nothing insincere.

The cold shoulder was more than Lauren could handle. She pounded her fist hard against the steering wheel, fuming. Giving up for the time being, she threw up a hand and started the engine while Constance simmered in hurt feelings. Lauren made a U-turn and pulled back into traffic. Constance's emotions boiled over; she wasn't done yet.

"You're right. You're too busy to even bother caring enough to hate me," she accused.

"Is that what this is all about, preteen angst?"

"Shows how little you do know me. I'm fourteen now. That

makes me a teenager."

"Oh, and you are fourteen. I am so impressed. And if you were to depart today, what a footprint you would have left on this planet. But how would I know? You and your father. You make such a nice pair. He is so great, I suppose. The always cheery, unread author. What a joke."

"Well, at least he doesn't cheat on you like you do on him," Constance blurted out.

Mortified, Lauren slammed the brakes at a yellow light turning to red. "What did you just say?"

"He knows. He's not stupid."

So he does know, she thought. *Fine. All the better.*

But it was an insincere thought. Lauren had prided herself on being crafty. She had thought she had covered all the bases. *How could Dennis have found out?* Putting that aside for the moment, she turned to Constance.

"This is an inappropriate conversation, and I'm certainly not going to discuss my personal business with you."

Constance didn't know whether her mother believed her or not. In reality, she was more suspicious of Lauren's activities than her forgiving father was. Either way, she was outmaneuvered and outmatched. Her mother had too many years and too much experience on her. However, she had started a chain reaction. She had stuck her neck out and was more than willing to stand by her convictions. Her pain flowed.

"Daddy still loves you, but you don't love him! You don't love either of us! Why didn't you just abort me if you didn't want me? Was I an *oops*, a mistake? Did you marry my father just so it wouldn't look bad being an unwed mother and you'd have someone to take care of me?"

The light turned green, but Lauren's foot remained firmly upon the brake.

Constance folded her arms across her chest. "Light's green."

Lauren just glared at her daughter.

A cacophony of car horns sounded as angry drivers were held up behind them. Lauren turned on her hazard lights in response.

Thinking maybe she had gone too far, Constance began biting her nails. Still, she believed what she said in frustration was truth. It needed to be said, and if her father wasn't going to address the subject, someone sure had to.

Cars began to maneuver around them. Angry drivers shouted unheard obscenities through their side windows at her. Lauren blocked them out. Her eyes were locked on Constance, and her foot was locked on the brake.

"Now you listen to me, young lady. I had you because I wanted you. I didn't have a doctor stick a vacuum cleaner up my vagina and suck you to oblivion. You remember that! Everything I do is so you can have the life you want, but that certainly doesn't include giving you the right to mouth off to me. Now, stop your damned whining about not being loved. You wanna know what not being loved is? What if I threw you out of this car, out of the house for that matter, and told you to go it alone? How long do you think those nice, designer clothes would last, being the only stitch of fabric you have with you?"

The light turned green, again, and still, she remained fixed.

"You think you've got it so bad," she continued, "You feel you need more love and affection, do you? You're fourteen, now. I breastfed you, changed your diapers, took you to the doctor's when you were sick. Fourteen! I guess that's old enough to understand the universal truth about life, kiddo. Nothing—*nothing*—is free. Got it? Every breath of air costs something. And that pop culture, pink paint—love and affection—isn't gonna get you through the world or pay the bills, sweetcakes."

"Yeah, don't I know it. But it sure would be nice," Constance pouted.

CHAPTER FIFTEEN

L auren's face was aglow in the bright beam of a singular desk lamp. It was exceedingly late, but she was about ready to call it a night. She was putting the finishing touches on closing arguments. As per her norm, Lauren glanced up at the grandfather clock—twelve-thirty. Oddly enough, amid the towers of files and law books, the family Bible, which had been collecting years of dust unopened, was spread open on a bookstand before her. Had someone else put it there? Had *He* been here? Lauren tried to remain focused on her work, but she found herself, more and more, glancing up and reading out of Proverbs.

The door to her den was also open, but not nearly as widely as the Good Book. There were three gentle knocks that she didn't acknowledge. Quietly, her husband, Dennis, pushed open the door and entered, holding in his hand a steaming cup of white tea— Lauren's favorite. Setting it down in front of her, he bent down and gently kissed his wife's forehead and stood patiently by her side.

Dennis Hill was a slender, intellectual type, complete with round, wire-rimmed glasses. He had a quiet serenity one might see in elderly, churchgoing women. Dennis hated confrontation of any kind. In fact, he would go out of his way to avoid it. Usually, he would blink his powder-blue eyes, profusely apologize, and walk away from anyone having even a minor conflict with him. It wasn't worth it to get angry. It accomplished little.

Because of his mild-mannered qualities, many people had decided that he was weak, a nerd missing only his pocket protectors. Dennis didn't see himself as macho, but in his own way, he was comfortable in his masculinity. He just believed it to be much better to walk away from confrontation than say or do something he would later regret.

Although she had once found those traits charming, over time Lauren grew to loathe the behavior in Dennis. She saw him as spineless, a jellyfish without the penetrating sting. Lauren felt she no longer wanted or needed a man who waited on her hand and foot and was good to her. She wanted a rugged man's man, a muscular individual who wasn't afraid to take chances and grab life by the balls.

"Here you go," Dennis said quietly, as he set the mug down.

It seemed to him, at first, that she was so deeply involved in her work that Lauren hadn't heard him. In point of fact, however, Lauren was purposely ignoring him. She liked being alone. *Why must he constantly bother the hell out of me?* she thought. Lauren raised her eyes above the computer screen and stared vacantly into the steam rising in wispy swirls, dissipating in the air-conditioned room.

Lauren could not concentrate if she wasn't comfortable. And she wasn't. Her husband's shadow loomed over her, and she could hear his breathing over the soothing swing of the pendulum in the clock. It was pissing her off. She sighed heavily. Seeing he wasn't taking the hint and going away, Lauren took off her reading glasses and looked up at him.

"Tea," he said.

Did he have to talk? Lauren produced a fake smile and

sarcastically told him she could see it was the kind she liked. Then, as an afterthought, she managed a short "Thanks."

Dennis knew their marriage was unraveling but felt powerless to salvage it. It took two to want to work things out, and it was clear to him she wanted no part of it on her end. She was only going through the motions. However, for all of the rudeness and bitter sarcasm, he couldn't help but feel the need to be close to her. He hopelessly loved her. It pained him to think she despised him, that no matter what he did, it wasn't good enough. She wouldn't speak to him. He realized she found him unattractive in many ways and no longer wanted the intimacy between a husband and wife, but he couldn't wrap his head around the fact that she loathed him to the point of not wanting even to speak civilly. Still, he tried.

"Closing arguments? Must always feel good to come to the end. When I'm writing—"

"Dennis, please," she interrupted.

"Sorry. I see you're using the Good Book."

Lauren looked up at him in confusion. Dennis pointed to the Bible.

"It's just there. Just open," she shrugged.

He leaned over, read a few lines. "Proverbs. Where the seven deadly sins are found. What's the name of that movie with Brad Pitt and Morgan Freeman? *Seven?*"

"Now how would I know?"

Shrugging off the sarcastic remark, Dennis carried on. "Yeah, I think that's it."

Lauren dismissed his words at first, then zoomed in on one. "Wait a minute, what's so deadly about 'em, huh?"

"I don't know, actually. Do I look like God?"

He didn't sound like God, but still. Lauren spun her chair around, studying him intently, waiting to see if it were some sort of weird communiqué and Dennis was going to shift into The

Almighty. After a tense moment, she was convinced her husband was simply her dweeb husband, so she said, "No. Certainly not. A little short."

Dennis was amused and a little confused by the line. He didn't know exactly how to respond to it, and he decided just to move on.

"So, how's the case? See you on TV practically every day. You look great. Everyone's saying he had to do it, but I'm not sure if the evidence is there. How do you feel about Maze's chances?"

"It's not a sport."

Dennis waved the white flag, throwing his hands up in an act of surrender. Done trying to communicate, he started walking toward the door. He was getting better. It had only taken him three minutes to realize he had overstayed his welcome. He was thinking he should have known he wasn't welcome the moment he set foot inside.

Suddenly, Lauren said something that stopped him in his tracks.

"Your daughter hates me."

Dennis turned to her, thinking, *If only her mother would come home earlier in the day and interact with her more often, maybe she wouldn't have that problem.*

"Our daughter, you mean."

"I believe that she would not agree to that."

"No. Not true. She did inform me you two had . . . words."

"Really? Is that all she said?"

"Yeah. Nothing specific, honestly. Just that—"

Lauren cocked her head to the side to show she was listening.

"Well, she just wants more attention, you know, motherly attention."

Dennis was frustrated with trying to make a bad situation more tolerable. However, as per his character, he let it slide off his back as if he were the proverbial duck in water. Reaching for the Bible, he said, "You don't mind if I—"

Lauren stopped his hand just as he was about to pick it up. "For what?"

"I dunno. It's there, right? You know how I am with books."

"Tell me about it. They're practically in every room."

"Like your clocks." Dennis pointed out.

He didn't mean for it to be a dig, but Lauren's negative attitude was getting on his last nerve. He immediately regretted it. "It kinda feels like it's calling to me. Strange. A divine calling, as if saying, 'Hey, ol' boy, take a look: good for the soul.'"

Lauren's ears perked. "Calling you? Like how? What do you mean, 'calling you?' Do you hear a voice beckoning you?"

"No, nothing like that. I don't hear voices or anything, if that's what you mean. Nobody actually hears—"

Lauren would never be able to explain to her husband that not only had she heard the Almighty God speak, but she had seen him as well. Lauren removed Dennis' hand from the Bible and interrupted. "I'm not done with it yet."

"I thought you were. Oh, okay." He backed away, hands up in a symbol of truce. "Hey, by the way, I talked to Mark today. He said he thinks he can get this latest book optioned for a movie. Can you believe it?"

Lauren was unimpressed.

"That's right, even before it's finished. You know Keith Tarmin? He recently got one of his books optioned by a Hollywood studio. Mark suggested I make a few dramatic changes, you know, a little more action and a bit more sex stuff between the pages to beef it up."

Lacing her reply with plenty of sarcasm, she half-heartedly congratulated him.

"Could mean some pretty decent money," Dennis offered.

Lauren knew the right thing to do was to encourage and say something positive for a change. However, she had already lost precious sleep time talking to Dennis about stuff that didn't interest her much—correction, not at all. Opting to take the low road, Lauren jumped down his throat.

"Can't you see I'm working here?"

"Yeah, yeah, honey. That's why I brought you the tea."

"Well, thanks, but let me finish up before I go insane, will you, please?"

Dennis turned and silently headed in the direction he had come in.

"Dennis?"

Obediently, he turned.

"She didn't mention anything specific?"

Dennis had to think a moment. "Who? Constance? No."

Lauren stared at him and picked up the cup of tea. By the lack of steam, she could tell it had cooled a great deal. She squeezed the teabag and discarded it in the saucer. Closing her eyes, she took a long, soothing sip, savored it.

"Ah, the tea is nice. Thank you."

Although saddened by the course the conversation had taken and the cold way his wife had spoken to him, Dennis still smiled. Half-brokenhearted, yet half warmed by the minuscule amount of affection, he left her to her work.

CHAPTER SIXTEEN

Darkness engulfed Maze. He dreaded the sunless portion of the calendar day. Those hours between sunset and dawn unnerved him. For many, night brought serenity; for him, it brought only madness. The slightest sound startled him. Sleep eluded him.

Maze had few supportive family members and even fewer friends. After the . . . unspeakable incident, everyone had seemed to scatter to the four winds. Only a handful wanted anything to do with him. Most had believed he was guilty long before the case even went to trial. His brother wouldn't talk to him. Neighbors went out of their way to avoid him. No phone calls. No letters. No messages. Nothing. He was virtually alone. Alone was not a happy place for the fragile mind of Mr. Maze.

Being in court and on a set schedule helped to a certain extent. At least there was noise. With his medication, Maze was able to keep himself somewhat together during much of the daylight hours. But when the sky turned from yellow to pink to a deep midnight blue, and Venus graced the western heaven, that's when things became more perilous. When all grew quiet in that part of the world and there was nothing to do to pass the time, his mind would play evil tricks on him. Quiet. He hated not having sound. It unnerved him, wreaked havoc on what little remained of his sanity. Maze was in a dark, dark place.

Tonight was the darkest night of them all. It droned on and on and on.

Maze lay in his bed and gazed out the curtainless window of his second-floor, red-brick apartment. Mercifully, there was light: manmade, but still most assuredly light. The streetlamp, just a few yards beyond his window, cast a long, near flawless, rectangular beam onto the beige carpeting just past the bedposts. If not for the small, jagged crack in the upper right corner of the beveled glass, it would have been perfection. Maze stared, but he wasn't actually seeing much of anything.

His mind tried to block any outside interference. Shrieks of *You're going to prison, loser* and *You know what they're gonna do to you, Maze* drifted to his ears from the street below. They had been almost a nightly occurrence for months leading up to the trial but had died down for the most part. Now that it was his last night of freedom, his tormentors had returned with a vengeance, shouting vicious obscenities at him. He hated them, but he fumed with the lights off, pretending not to be home. They kept trying, hoping to say the right words to get Maze to explode. He didn't take the bait. Too many of them to fight off. He drifted off into a dreamlike trance, his stare vacant, as if many hours and miles away from the hustle and bustle of the City of Angels and the fate, favorable or unfavorable, which awaited him.

Although he had taken his prescribed sleep-aid medication hours earlier, Maze was not able to shut down his overactive imagination enough to become drowsy. No matter what he did or how hard he tried, sleep eluded him. So be it. Like every other inconvenience in his life, he simply dealt with it. Insomnia had been a constant, clinging companion for months, and although he felt that he should be used to it by now, he wasn't. It drained him both physically and emotionally. Of all the distractions, inconveniences, and problems he faced, sleep deprivation was the one aggravation most difficult to overcome.

Insomnia was debilitating, but he had no other recourse than to tolerate it, to endure it as one would a bothersome neighbor mowing their lawn at seven on a Saturday morning or a chronic, nagging ache from which there was no relief. However, Maze was far from a state of what one would call acceptance. It was his burden to bear. He bore it as he had on other nights. Tonight was not dissimilar to the night before or the night before that, or even the night before that. In fact, it was virtually a carbon copy of nearly every night since *the event.*

Just thinking about his wife's death increased his heart rate. It was elevated at that very moment. He could feel the rapid pounding within his chest cavity. Maze thought briefly about popping another anxiety pill; he even plucked the tiny vial off his nightstand but then ultimately decided against it. In his despair, he hoped the pressure on his most vital organ would, at some point before dawn, cause a vapor lock and put an end to his miserable existence.

Sweat beaded on his forehead and then snaked its way down his creased brow and cheeks in mini-rivulets, soaking his pillow. Consumed with somber, despairing visions, Maze was a pathetic, tortured soul. Random thoughts and pictures of the past—mostly unpleasant ones—flashed before his mind's eye in rapid succession.

Intermittently, those hurtful images were then replaced with visions of the as-yet-undecided court proceedings a few hours from now. *Closing arguments. The last day!* Maze wasn't at all confident. He glanced at the clock, the only piece decorating the nightstand, a scratched-up, water-stained relic from the 1960s. The digital timepiece was facing away from him. Maze picked it up and held it in front of him. *2:06*. He set it on the bed next to him and deliberately pushed it to the floor.

Since Amanda's death, Maze had taken great pains to rid his life of practically every piece of furniture, clothing item, linen, cookware, and knickknack from their place. He had two reasons. First, he needed to liquidate nearly everything in his possession to retain his high-profile lawyer. Second and more importantly, it was what he needed to do for his own sanity. Everything reminded him of the past—his past—with Amanda. He had thought that after ridding his life of those mementos, things would get better. It was the furthest from the truth. His tortured mind always played back moments when his wife's sophisticated presence graced the house. Without her, it was no longer a home, just a lonely house, a temporary place to crash until either his lease was up or he was found guilty and sent to prison to live out the remainder of his wretched days.

Although Lauren tried to assure him he would be found innocent, nothing was certain. He saw how the jury looked at him; he knew what they thought about him. It wasn't the way people looked at a poor fella having to endure such pain and humiliation on top of losing his beloved wife. In his mind, it was a "burn in hell, you murderer" kind of stare. The mere thought sent a shiver through him.

Now, as he lay atop the bare mattress on the rickety old bed he had recently purchased from the thrift store on Tenth Street, he could not help but remember the beautiful, flower-print drapes that had once covered the window, keeping out the glow of the streetlight. He remembered how much that streetlight used to bother him. It no longer did. After sunset, it was the only light in his life. As he lay in bed locked in worrisome reflection, sleep was the furthest thing from his mind. It was then he realized the voices outside his window had mercifully ceased.

It was quiet, chillingly quiet.

The cooling unit inside the refrigerator in the small galley kitchen came on, startling him back to reality. *The kitchen.* The thought of what it looked like depressed him even further. It certainly wasn't how Amanda had kept it. *Untidy* wasn't the word he would have used to describe its state of uncleanliness. The sink was piled high to the simple light fixture mounted on the wall above it with several weeks' worth of unwashed dishes. The plastic garbage can was filled beyond overflowing, and the countertops were splattered with the decaying, moldy remains of meager dinners past. If not for the underlying stench of decay that permeated the atmosphere, the colors would have reminded him of an artist's studio. He didn't even want to look at the disgusting, stuck-on goop inside the microwave. The door would barely open and close because of the sticky residue on it.

Maze took no enjoyment out of life and had no motivation to do much of anything productive. If he were found guilty, he rationalized, someone else would have the unenviable job of scraping and disinfecting these things.

Trying to shake the demons disrupting the normal transfer of electrical impulses in his brain, Maze rolled to his right and reached for the remote sitting on the other, matching nightstand. He wasn't necessarily in the mood to watch TV, but he needed the distraction. *Maybe,* he thought, *there will be something on that will put me to sleep.*

Maze clicked the on button. A single, blue dot formed in the center of the old box television, followed by a thin, bright, white line as it hummed and struggled to life. At least he had cable. Soon, ESPN's *Sport's Center* came into view. He watched as the two announcers discussed and summarized game four of the Eastern Conference finals between the Cleveland Cavaliers and Atlanta Hawks. After the decisive win, LeBron and company were in command with a three to one lead in the best-of-seven series. The fans behind them who had stayed to see the commentary and hopefully get a few seconds on camera were cheering and holding signs. Having King James back in a trade from Miami had helped the team immensely. The bitter taste left in the city's mouth after LeBron's shocking departure was formally forgotten.

Normally, Maze would have been glued to the screen. He was a huge fan of basketball. But with his fate in the hands of twelve angry jurors, he had lost interest in just about everything. He figured, *What's the point?* He began channel surfing. Basketball, a sitcom rerun, commercial, commercial . . .

Suddenly, the screens stopped flipping. Maze's finger had slipped off the remote control and what he saw made his eyes widen in amazement. It could not have been a coincidence. An evangelical minister was holding up a Bible in his right hand. He was preaching on guilt, conviction, and atonement of sins. It was exactly what he needed when he needed it. Maze lowered the remote to the bed. He sat bolt upright and listened intently to the preacher's bold sermon, transfixed, even mesmerized, for hours.

Mercifully, the sky began to lighten: the dawning of a new, cloudless day in Southern California. Although he hadn't slept, Maze hopped out of bed refreshed and rejuvenated, Bible in hand. He washed, splashed on some Aqua Velva Musk, and dressed in a pair of gray sweats and a sleeveless undershirt. *Wifebeater undershirt,* he thought. He laughed nervously at the irony of it. It was the first time he had been able to produce a laugh in a very long time. It felt exhilarating. It felt like freedom! Maze knew it was inappropriate, but still, it felt good.

Taking pen in hand, Maze wrote a short thank-you letter to Reverend Jason Evens and filled out a check in the minuscule amount of twenty-three dollars, all he had left to his embattled name. The chains had been loosed. He was free, liberated from the encumbrances of his thoughts, his self-loathing. Maze sealed the envelope, placed the second to last stamp in the corner, and placed it in the outgoing mailbox.

Maze had much cleaning to do before court. He turned the fan on, placed it on the seat of a chair, and faced it toward the kitchen. The strong breeze only succeeded in blowing the stench around the apartment. He opened the three windows and cheerfully went to work. Grabbing a large, plastic pail from under the sink, he put a couple of capfuls of Lysol inside, thought about it a moment, then added a couple more. Whistling an old Santana tune, he placed the pail under the faucet in the bathroom, filled it with hot water, and tossed a new sponge into it. Then he carried it back to his filthy kitchen and immediately started.

For the first time in months, Maze was at peace, content in the knowledge projected to him by God through the televangelist. His spirits were elevated to new heights. After hearing an enlightening sermon, he was confident things were going to be all right. What the preacher had conveyed to him could not have been mere coincidence. He was convinced the entire message was meant for him.

Maze realized he had lost track of time. He went into the bedroom and picked up his alarm clock. 7:47. Wrapped up in his chores, he had spent a great deal longer disinfecting the kitchen than he had planned. Washing the caked-on residue off the walls was just going to have to wait for a more opportune time. Maze had to fly. He had less than half an hour before Ryan would be knocking at his door to pick him up and take him to court. Maze wanted to be waiting for him when he did.

Ryan Thompson was always prompt and pulled up to the curb at 8:15 sharp. Maze was sitting on the stoop of the apartment complex, reading from the Bible. Ryan pushed a button to lower the driver's side window.

"Good morning, Maze."

Maze stood but said nothing, a cheerful look on his face.

Ryan noticed. "Ah, you too, huh? Reading the Bible."

"I had a vision," Maze blurted.

Ignoring Maze's interruption, Ryan added, "Did you sleep better last night? Pills help you at all?"

Maze got into the passenger seat. "I didn't sleep," he said, beaming. "I had a vision."

Ryan found Maze's smile disconcerting. In fact, it creeped him out.

Maze pressed on. "Did you hear what I said, Mr. Thompson? I had a vision. I had a profound, life-altering vision."

Ryan simply shifted into first gear and sped away, arriving at the courthouse without having said a word.

Later, Maze was sitting on a wooden bench outside the courtroom, alone. He was skimming through his Bible when Lauren walked up to him. She asked Maze if he knew where Ryan had gone off to. Other than dropping Maze off at his apartment before heading to his own home, Ryan wasn't supposed to let him out of his sight for five seconds, for Maze's own protection as much as to guard against a flight risk. After all, Maze had shown nothing but erratic behavior all through the case, and there was no telling what he might do to himself if he were left on his own. Maze simply shrugged and went back to reading the passage of Scripture. Lauren did a shrug of her own, deciding she would address her colleague's absence later.

Ryan was disgusted with his charge and had already made his way inside, along with many spectators and news media. After all the nonsense Maze had been telling him about visions on the way to court, Ryan no longer cared what happened to him.

Lauren focused on the task at hand. She turned to Maze and smiled.

"Sun is up. Birds are singing. Gonna be a hell of a day for a nail-in-the-coffin closing argument."

Maze looked up. "Ms. Hill, I had a vision last night."

A queasy feeling came over Lauren. Dread immediately replaced her cheerful confidence. Cautiously looking around, she said, "Let's keep the visions to a minimum today, shall we?"

Maze didn't understand exactly what his defense attorney meant by that. He hadn't informed her of any other visions or even had any others. Why had she said *today*? Maybe the word had been inadvertently added. Still, the peculiar way in which she was looking around, as if expecting God to appear, was unsettling.

Lauren started to head into the courtroom, expecting her client to follow obediently in her footsteps; however, he remained seated. As she was about to open the door, he said, "God spoke to me."

Lauren froze in her tracks and glanced down at her watch. *8:53*. Court would be starting in a matter of minutes. She rushed to Maze and practically dragged him into an empty courtroom.

As soon as the door closed, she asked, "What do you mean, God spoke to you?"

"I had a vision."

"What did He look like?"

"I don't want to be found guilty."

"You won't. Now, what did He look like?"

"Deuteronomy 19:15."

Exasperated, Lauren practically screamed. "Tell me what you saw, damn it!"

Maze paged through the Bible. "I must read this to you. *'One witness is not enough to convict anyone accused of any crime or offense they may have committed. A matter must be established by the testimony of two or three witnesses.'*" Maze looked up at Lauren. "There are no witnesses against me, just like you've been saying. No witnesses."

Lauren rolled her eyes. "Get to the point!"

Maze lowered his gaze and continued reading. "'*You must purge the evil from among you. The rest of the people will hear of this and be afraid, and never again will such an evil thing be done among you. Show no pity: life for life, eye for eye, tooth for tooth, hand for hand, foot for foot.'*"

"Look, we don't have time for this. Why are you reading this to me?"

"I see, now. I see clearly. Evil is trying to crucify me. I'm ready to win. I won't be afraid anymore. I won't squirm in guilt."

Lauren thought, *Now? Now, on the last day, you're going to behave like a good little defendant?* But she kept those hurtful words to herself. Still, she could have cared less about what he read. What Lauren needed to know was what in heaven's name Maze had seen and she wasn't going anywhere until he told her, even though she knew by now they must be late for entry to the courtroom. She tried a different tactic.

"Listen, all I care about is that you don't stand up or speak out of turn, got it? I'll run the show."

Maze nodded then carried on. "I want you to know, though, I truly loved my wife. Loved her. It wasn't perfect between us, but it was love."

"I believe you." Even if she didn't, Lauren knew it was the prudent thing to say.

After a reflective beat, Maze spoke. "It was her time, just her time. Ecclesiastes 3:1—*'For everything, there is a season, and a time for every matter under heaven: a time to be born, and a time to die.'*"

"Okay, so you've read the Bible. Is that supposed to impress me?"

"I had a vision. He showed me," Maze reiterated.

"We've established that point, now." *Wait a minute,* she thought. Something new had been added to his previous statement. *Showed.* "He did? What did He look like, his features?" She grabbed him by the lapels of his rumpled suit.

"I'm not a stupid man, Ms. Hill."

Lauren released him from her grip.

"It was all on TV," he continued. "A televangelist. Just an evangelist, but I know he came with the Spirit of God."

Lauren rolled her eyes. She had jeopardized her career again for this? *A laughable televangelist, a mortal of questionable character?*

Maze continued. "Everything lined up for me. It was like something calling me, telling me to turn on the television and see what I saw, hear what I heard, and then, read what I read. The guilt was too much to bear, the guilt that she was gone. I needed strength. I have it now. I have that strength. You're right. *Win.* Let's win this. That's why I even sent them what little money I have left. Like a wishing well. I needed faith to ride out the storm. Thank God that there is a god."

The only thing Lauren fully understood was that she had wasted her time for nothing. Controlling her temper, she shook his shoulder and brusquely said, "C'mon, we have to go. It's showtime!"

CHAPTER SEVENTEEN

L auren Hill looked at her watch before entering the courtroom. Relief. Until that moment, she had been trying to come up with a half-baked excuse as to why she and her client were running behind. As it had turned out, she didn't have to—

Wait a minute, she thought. *That's impossible!* She knew more than just a few agonizing minutes had elapsed while Maze rambled incessantly about visions and televangelists in the adjacent courtroom. Much more. Lauren worked it in her head several times, coming up with the same answer each time. She and Maze had been conversing for upward of fifteen minutes.

How the hell did we gain . . . ? her thought trailed off. Deep down, she knew the answer, but she didn't want to admit it. She was trying to put the previous day behind her and forget it had even happened. It seemed God wasn't going to allow that. Yep, there could be only one explanation for what had taken place. "This isn't happening," she said. Lauren placed a trembling hand upon her forehead, pressing down on the bridge of her nose as if she could press the truth down. She grew angry with herself, with circumstances, and most of all, with God. He, or some strange phenomenon, was messing with her head.

Working the simple math, she and Maze should have been walking in ten minutes past the hour, more than enough reason to be chastened for her lack of punctuality. One or two minutes would not have mattered and would likely have been overlooked as a simple miscalculation on her part. But ten or more? Given what happened the previous day, no way would Judge Howell let it go unnoticed.

He must still be here, she thought. *But where?* There was no time to think about it. She had to pull herself together. Judge Howell was not going to allow her to crack like yesterday.

In a twisted way, Lauren wished her client had seen the same visions she had. Even from an emotionally fragile sap like him, any validation would help her believe she was not winding down the dark road to Insanity, USA. That, in and of itself, would have softened the blow and made the likely reprimand from Judge Howell well worth it. Maze couldn't give her this help, however. Those visions were truly for her eyes only.

A strange, foreboding feeling came over her. Her legs suddenly grew weak and shaky, as if about to buckle. She gripped the doorknob for support and told Maze, standing next to her erect and beaming with confidence for the first time all trial, to enter without her.

"I can't allow this. Nothing is going to come between me and sweet victory," she whispered. Straightening, she completely blocked the unexplainable time discrepancy from her mind. She grit her teeth. "Not this day." She looked up at the ceiling and far beyond, mockingly saying, "Thanks, God, I owe ya one."

"Are you okay, Ms. Hill?"

Lauren looked up at the kindly older gentleman offering assistance to her. "Fine. Just a headache, that's all." She gently brushed him aside and entered the courtroom.

Both counsel and client took their respective seats as the last few stragglers entered behind them. A flash caused Lauren's eyes to widen. *Is it God?* She looked up and saw the bronze relief of The Great Seal of California glistening in the rays of the eternal sun. Relief! *Pull yourself together, Lauren.*

Lauren was mesmerized by the light dancing before her eyes. With great effort, she willed herself to look away. Glowing round spots filled her field of vision as she tried to focus on her notes. Spectral colors danced before her eyes, distorting her vision. Clearly, she had been staring too long at the brightness. She closed her eyes and waited until the multitude of colors blinked out on the dark background of the inside of her eyelids. *This, too, shall pass. But please, no more visions. Not today.*

Almost immediately after the last seat had been occupied, the room once again filled, the bailiff called everyone to order.

"All rise. Honorable Susan Howell presiding." A dramatic hush swept over the courtroom as Judge Howell walked toward the bench.

"Be seated."

Her vision clearing, Lauren chuckled to herself. *Honorable, my ass*, she thought. *The woman's a bonafide lush. Gone through enough Crown Royal to fill Lake Superior—twice. It's a wonder the wrinkled prune has any liver left.* It relaxed her to indulge in those nasty thoughts.

Lauren glanced at the jury. All twelve were still attentive, still diligent, even after four long days of often heated debate. They were adjusting their chairs and flipping open pads of paper in preparation for taking notes. Out of the corner of her eye, she could see Bradley staring at her with longing before finally turning back to shuffling through his prepared note cards. Lauren fought the urge to look back at him and was relieved when he turned away.

For the first time in five days, Maze sat tall and straight, eager to get the trial over with. He emanated strength and self-assurance. Lauren and Ryan looked at each other, surprised.

"Must be the pills," Ryan said.

Both lawyers were content with the outward changes, although Ryan wondered when Maze's meds were going to wear off. From there, he felt, it would only be a matter of time before he would revert to his old self. He was still disgusted with Maze's fabricated stories.

Lauren, on the other hand, was confident after having spoken to Maze. Whatever the man had heard or saw on TV had somehow altered his way of thinking. That was fine with her. As long as he wasn't disruptive or belligerent, she could care less what he thought he saw.

She turned to the prosecution table, now catching a glimpse of Bradley's still wandering eye. He smiled at her, but she quickly turned her head. His smile was comforting to her, but she could not figure out what to do about her feelings or if she honestly needed to worry about them at all. *Maybe they will take care of themselves, in time.*

Judge Howell settled into her seat and faced the prosecution. "Mr. Bradley, are you prepared to start?"

Standing, he affirmed he was and approached the jury.

"May it please the court, ladies and gentlemen of the jury, my name is Dillon Bradley, as I'm sure you are aware. This is my first formal opportunity to address you directly. On behalf of everyone on the prosecution team, those working diligently side-by-side with me, Mr. Jack Osterman, Miss Sarah Fields, and Mr. William Robinson, I would like to begin by thanking each and every one of you for the time and attention you've put into this case."

Ryan leaned toward Lauren with a wry smile. "You gonna thank me like that, too?"

"Thompson, I wouldn't thank you if the world was under nuclear attack and you had built me a bomb shelter complete with a Jacuzzi and swimming pool."

Ryan lowered his head to the table to contain his laughter. Lauren was about to scold him for leaving Maze alone in the hallway earlier, but just then, in her right ear, she heard, "Why don't you thank him?"

Lauren's self-satisfied smile died as fear overtook her. She had heard that voice far too often as of late. The stern, logical words of the Living God filled her hearing. Lauren gripped the edge of the table and froze.

The now familiar likeness of God—the only form in which The Almighty had chosen to reveal Himself to her—was comfortably sitting in a chair next to her, hands loosely clasped around the knee of His crossed legs. He looked relaxed, casual. Gently bouncing His leg up and down, God didn't seem to have a care in the world. *He even thought to bring His Own chair,* she noted.

This time, she wasn't thinking those thoughts mockingly. It was more a nervous musing, as one would think when laughing inappropriately during a tragedy. Inside, she wasn't laughing. She was frightened out of her wits. Either she was both legally and legitimately certifiable, or God was truly trying to unravel her. Neither option appealed to her.

Lauren scanned the room. From what was taking place around her, it was clear that no one else saw the divine manifestation. Everyone was engrossed in Bradley's closing arguments. As much as she was hoping others could see what she saw and react accordingly, the vision was solely for her bewildered eyes only.

Lauren turned to face God. As she knew He would be, The Lord was impeccably dressed in a divinely dapper, metallic-looking three-piece suit. It shimmered with the slightest movement. She was certain the strange material did not exist anywhere on planet Earth. The way it flashed and danced in the brightly lit courtroom, it seemed to move fluidly upon him, as if the fabric wasn't fabric at all. Maybe it wasn't. As she stared, mesmerized by it, the suit seemed to be alive.

God smiled, a kindly, almost vacant smile, giving the impression He was not in the present, but instead pondering the direction He should take or musing over an event from the distant past. As gratifying as it was having one of the opposite sex gaze in her general direction without gawking at her assets, at the same time it was a bit unnerving. She wasn't accustomed to it. God's sparkling aquamarine eyes looked a million miles away. She could have sworn they were sky blue the last time she saw him.

It was refreshingly different, an intimidating kind of intriguing, but only at first. The longer she looked at God, the more she understood He saw her as being of no real consequence, an insignificant speck in the greater universe. He sighed as if impatiently waiting for an opponent to make the next move in a painstaking game of chess. Never had a man reacted to her with such disinterest. It was as if He were bored to death with her. Yes, that was most definitely the term—*bored!* He casually picked a small piece of lint off of His jacket.

Blessed. He said I should consider myself blessed. Although He had never spoken to her in anything other than a loving fashion, Lauren did not feel *blessed* at that moment. She was terrified.

Lauren shifted her gaze to the woman on the bench. Seeing the movement, the judge stared back. Nothing seemed amiss. Judge Howell was still Judge Howell. Of course she was. God was seated next to her. What did she expect? Lauren turned to Him, then back to the bench. The judge looked at her, puzzled.

Lauren felt as if there were nowhere to turn. She was being studied as if she were a patient in a psych ward. It didn't help her fragile state. Back and forth, Lauren looked between God and Judge Howell. The longer she did, the more the walls closed in. Closer and closer they drew. *No. No. This isn't happening,* she mouthed.

Judge Howell looked with concern at the increasingly anxious defense counsel. Why Ms. Hill was turning her head nervously back and forth between her and the prosecution's table, she couldn't say. There didn't seem to be anything to cause such a reaction. After Lauren's bizarre behavior the day before, Judge Howell seriously began to question Lauren's sanity. Everyone has a breaking point, and it looked as if Ms. Hill had reached hers.

I knew I should have called an ambulance yesterday, she thought.

Truth be told, Judge Howell was secretly rooting for Hill in this instance, and not just because of Hill's usual competence and the challenges facing a working woman. The prosecution's case was built upon circumstantial evidence and speculative conjecture, and Judge Howell knew it. Juries, however, were fickle. *Come on, Lauren, keep it together a few more hours. Your client needs you.*

From across the courtroom, the prosecutor's voice rose as his cadence quickened. "Martin Maze is a murderer of the worst kind. Cold-blooded, ruthless. Ask yourselves, 'Where is his wife?'"

Lauren heard little. She was fighting hard but felt herself slipping further and further. Unable to grasp the presence of God, she spiraled. She coughed loudly and then whispered into Ryan's ear, telling him to hold the fort a moment. She pushed back her chair, which scraped across the floor, and stood.

Looking up at her, flabbergasted, Ryan held out his hands in confusion.

He was too late to stop her. Lauren coolly walked down the center aisle and through the doors in the back of the courtroom.

Watching her go, Maze seemed somewhat deflated. "Where's she going?"

Although he needed reassuring himself, Ryan flashed his pearly whites and told Maze his lawyer would return shortly. Maze didn't seem at all comforted by Ryan's evasive answer, but what could he do? Maybe he could have fired her, maybe not. It hardly mattered anyway, since the vision of last night had reassured him everything would turn out in his favor.

Watching his adversary leave, Bradley continued as if this sort of thing happened all the time.

"Either Amanda Maze was a world-class swimmer, or she is in a watery grave. It has already been established she was not a world-class swimmer. I believe that is all you need to know about this case."

Eyes forward, Lauren bolted down the corridor to the women's restroom. She couldn't look behind her, didn't dare to. If she saw Him, Lauren was afraid the last remaining thread of her sanity would snap. She never believed it, never thought it was conceivable, but the adage that there was a fate worse than death was true. She wished she were dead. Scared out of her mind, she began hyperventilating. *Why? Why is this happening to me?* she wondered. On the verge of tears, she picked up her pace. At least the hounds hadn't tried to follow her this time. She flung open the door to the ladies' bathroom and dashed inside, slamming the door behind her.

Panting, Lauren went directly to the sinks. She placed her hands on the middle basin and turned on the cold water. Something was dreadfully wrong. She began to shake. This was no Los Angeles earthquake; the unwelcome trembling was coming from within. At first, she thought she might be having a seizure. It became difficult to remain upright. Her legs were giving out. Looking down at her trembling hands, she felt extremely weak. "Concentrate, Lauren!" she scolded herself.

Catching a glimpse of herself in the mirror, Lauren was appalled at the reflection staring back at her. She didn't look as disheveled and pathetic as she had the day before: her make-up was intact. However, she looked every bit as scared as she felt, as if she were on the verge of collapsing.

Lauren reached for a paper towel and ran it under the water. She closed her eyes and placed the cool, damp cloth over them.

It had the desired effect. A few seconds later, she removed the soothing paper and focused on the reflective surface in front of her. "Mirrors are so cruel," she said aloud. "They never lie."

Then, there He was. One second, He was not there, the next, standing behind her in the chrome and glass was the unmistakable reflection of the Almighty.

Lauren quickly spun around, as much to confront her nemesis as to confirm His existence. She was definitely not seeing things. "God!"

He smiled but remained silent.

Fear left her, replaced immediately with controlled anger. "What are you doing in the ladies' bathroom? You can't come in here."

"No?" He snickered.

"No! If you have to go, the men's room is down the hall," she pointed.

God laughed heartily.

It did sound ridiculous. In spite of everything, Lauren chuckled. But that small emotional display cracked her barriers. "No, no, no. This isn't happening!" She turned off the faucet and closed her eyes. Soon, her own faucets started. "This is nuts. I'm fucking nuts." She tried desperately to calm herself, but once the first tear dribbled down her cheek, there was no stopping them.

God approached and wiped away her tears. Even though His presence was the reason she was freaking out, His touch was comforting. Lauren's tears dried immediately.

God knew what she needed to hear, even if it was totally off topic. "Lauren, your mother did not see or hear the Virgin Mary."

Lauren calmed. Her breathing slowed to normal, a perfect twelve breaths per minute.

"But you are indeed hearing and seeing me. This, I can assure you," He paused. "I am not a figment of your imagination. This is true reality—reality beyond that of what you think you know.

Do not minimize this experience or opportunity."

Questions flooded her. "What opportunity?"

"To pour out your heart. You see, and yet you continue to marvel."

"Oh, gawd!"

God took exception to His name being taken in vain and opened His mouth to speak.

"I know, I know," she said, holding up a manicured hand. "Please, don't say anything. Just an expression." Then she added, "Oh, my gawd, what the hell am I saying. I'm certifiable, I'm 5150! I think I'm talking to God. I'm yelling at God. What God? Oh, gawd! Why is this happening!"

All the while, Lauren was pacing back and forth. When finished with her tirade, she checked the door. No one was coming in. It was just her and the Almighty, and He wasn't at all happy.

"Do not trifle with Me, Lauren."

The room shook as the full weight of his words crashed down upon her. He now had her undivided attention.

Continuing calmly, God said, "Ours is a business of love and compassion, not a trivial one of this or that, come and go, or here and there. Do you deny me? My existence? If so, you only deny yourself of the abundant fruit of rapturous joy. *Crazy* is everything outside this Holy Communion. Be not confused or scared, but at peace, Lauren. You are assuredly not insane."

Lauren was overwhelmed with dark memories of her mother. Tears flowed freely again. "When I saw her, when I saw my mother, she would babble and call me."

"Fear not. You are not your mother."

"But I don't understand you. I don't want to be insane . . . but I don't understand what's happening."

God waved a hand. Lauren's tears dried, instantly. She couldn't open to His thoughts and teachings in such an unproductive state.

"Be determined to trust Me. Then, in turn, you will be able to trust yourself. Abstain from all sin, but especially lust. Be ethical and honest. Do not try to deceive or give false hope to anyone. Know you have limitations. Do not puff yourself up with pride. And do not hurt the feelings of others."

Lauren absorbed His words and looked down at her shoes. A wave of conviction washed over her. It was now all coming together. Lauren was about to say her last line of the play and the theater would fill with applause. But there was momentary silence. She was going to say something. Tell God she understood and apologize for her sinful ways.

The door Lauren was leaning against was suddenly pushed from the outside. God disappeared. Lauren moved aside, and a tall woman entered. Seeing Lauren's misery, the woman asked if she was okay.

Wiping her tears, Lauren unconvincingly said she was.

Not buying it, the woman dug through her large purse. "Here you go," she said, handing Lauren a pack of tissues. "Take the whole pack."

Before she could change her mind, Lauren did. Then, looking at her watch, she produced a smile. Once again, God had slowed time. Looking up, she said, "I owe you another one."

CHAPTER EIGHTEEN

For Lauren Hill, closing arguments were more than a mere summary of the evidence or the last chance to impress upon a weary jury the enormity of the prosecution's burden of proof. She found only limited satisfaction in persuading them that enough reasonable doubt had been established to find the defendant not guilty. What she loved was the occasion to perform, to speak at great length without interruption on a grand stage. It was like being on Broadway, but without the hot spotlights and demanding audiences. A crowded courtroom afforded her the opportunity to strut her stuff, show off her extensive vocabulary and honed speaking ability, while verbally thrashing her opponent for lack of preparation and proof. Normally, she thrived on the intensity, the pressure of being in the limelight. It was gratifying. It was electrifying. It was titillating. All that had changed this time, however, and she was visibly rattled.

But no matter how nervous she might be, it was nearly showtime.

Judge Howell glared at Lauren as she quietly walked into the courtroom and took her seat. From the scowl on the judge's face, Lauren knew the woman running the show was not pleased with her behavior.

Judge Howell had been lenient with Lauren because of her gender, because she saw the enormous strain she had been under, and because, up until yesterday, she had presented a phenomenal case for her client's acquittal. However, everyone had a job to perform, and she expected it to be done to the letter. It was a system of laws, a system of order, and Lauren was disrupting that delicate balance. It no longer mattered to her what was going on inside that overworked head of hers. As much as she admired Lauren, she could not tolerate another interruption.

Looking up from his notes, Bradley cast a perturbed look at her before continuing. "The defense would like you to believe there is reasonable doubt! In the last few months of their marriage, how many times had the police visited the Maze address because of domestic violence issues? Seven!"

Martin Maze slapped the table. Lauren saw that her client was on the verge of not being able to hold up his end of the bargain and switched seats with Ryan.

"That's right," Bradley continued. "Seven times police responded to their residence because of excessive screaming and dishes breaking."

Seeing his displeasure, Lauren leaned into Maze's ear, "Listen to me—"

"It's not true."

"It is true," she scolded.

"But he's twisting it."

"Of course he is. What didn't you get from our previous conversation?"

"I loved my wife."

"I know it, and the jury knows it. I haven't had my turn."

Bradley held up his papers. "And here are the reports. An entire stack of them."

"I want him to stop," Maze begged.

This got her fired up. She had all but forgotten the incident in the restroom. "Listen to me! This is a contest, a competition. Do you understand? That's what court is, a place where two combatants do battle."

Lauren gripped his chin and turned his face to her. Everyone in the courtroom witnessed her frustrated reaction. Even Bradley, in the middle of his statement, noticed the circus show at the defense table.

"Two combatants," Lauren continued, "clothed in naked ambition meet in a staged setting designed to twist logic. That is what we do. We twist logic, stretch the truth into adjudged facts and have rendered a prejudice certitude."

Bradley cleared his throat and elevated his tone of voice. "Each of these reports states that Amanda Maze feared her husband would become violent toward her and cause injury."

"That's what I do," Lauren continued, whispering. "And I am the best at it. You don't need to get upset, stand up, or shout obscenities, and we don't need the Bible to win."

Maze looked at Lauren as if she had just committed blasphemy. As if he were a child facing a bully, he clutched the book tightly and held it close to his chest. "I don't want to be found guilty. The word of God brings me comfort."

"You're not guilty. We don't need your antics, the word of God, or the truth," she whispered. "What we do have are twelve marginally educated citizens of the City of Angels and a whole heck of a lot of statutes. It's been more than enough to find in your favor." Lauren let go of his face.

Maze swallowed. "You sure?"

"What is it you want me to do? If this book," she said, taking the Bible, "is helping you with your anxiety, then embrace it. Let its pages save your skin and your soul."

For all of his apprehensions, Maze was truly impressed with

her confident words, although, in the back of his mind, he knew it was best to err on the side of caution. Maze took back the Bible and opened to the bookmark on Proverbs. "Watch out! Proverbs 6:16. The Seven Deadly Sins. First of all, pride. It always precedes a fall."

Horrified, but trying to show it, Lauren took the book and gently closed it. How was it possible Maze was trying to show her exactly the same lesson God had been teaching her? No way could it have been a mere coincidence. Could this be God's way of reinforcing His wisdom? It may very well have been the final warning. She wasn't sure what kind of chastisement He might resort to next, and she was now concerned.

Bradley was finished with his closing arguments and took his seat at the prosecution's table. He had taken up nearly every minute of time allotted him. The rest of the team huddled around to congratulate him on his courtroom prowess.

All eyes were then fixated on Lauren.

But for all her shaken confidence, once Lauren Hill stood and started to give her prepared speech, the woman was on fire. She performed beautifully, conducting a symphony of words. The jurors, who had been questioning her ability as well as her sanity since yesterday, questioned no longer. They listened intently to her as she reiterated detailed arguments in such a way as to make them sound fresh and new.

"Amanda Maze had a known history of mental illness. She had been diagnosed as being bipolar and having borderline personality disorder. Her medical records attest to that fact. Furthermore, each of you has heard sworn testimony from Amanda's doctor. He had prescribed a plethora of medications, including antidepressants and lithium. Doctor Barrett testified that it had taken several months to get the dosages adjusted correctly." Lauren paused. "Mr. Maze loved his wife. I repeat: he *loved* her. He stayed with her despite her severe illness. He was married to her for five years. Yes, we don't deny that those were turbulent years, however, that turbulence was brought on by Amanda's mental instability."

The deceased's grieving mother burst into tears. Bradley turned, dramatically patted her hand for show, and offered her his condolences for the cold and callous way Lauren had presented her daughter to the jury.

Judge Howell was tired of having to bang the gavel, but at least this time it wasn't directed toward the defense table.

Turning to her client, Lauren saw Maze motioning for her to *tell them*. Without missing a beat, however, she walked over to Maze and, without looking down, casually opened the Bible for him. Then she poured herself a glass of water and, spinning around, walked deliberately to the jury and began to address them directly. "And that lovely cruise was a gift," she continued. "A gift from a loving husband to an adored wife. A time for them to spend together, allowing her to forget and leave her major troubles behind." Lauren glanced down at her notes and continued. "No, Amanda Maze was not a 'world-class swimmer,' if by 'world-class' the prosecution means she'd been in the Olympics or something. However, she most certainly could swim, as her mother testified."

Lauren started walking back toward the defense table, motioning for Ryan to pour another glass of water. Obediently, he had it for her before she arrived. Every move, every subtle gesture, was calculated. Sure, she had notes, but pausing to hydrate gave Lauren the opportunity to gather her thoughts and get the words precisely the way they needed to be said to impress the jury. Bradley still had the last word, and Lauren wanted to make sure whatever he had to say was inconsequential. By the time Bradley took the floor in rebuttal, she wanted to ensure that she and the twelve were on the same page and they would deliver a "not guilty" verdict.

Lauren took a few, dainty sips to wet her whistle, and turned once more to the jury. They were attentive. "Let's see. We know that on several occasions through her adult life, Mrs. Maze had contemplated suicide. In his testimony, even her ex-husband mentioned one particular incident in which she had held a knife to herself."

Some members of the jury jotted notes while several others leaned to converse with one another in inaudible whispers. It seemed they had been reminded of an important detail. It further seemed that Lauren had them eating out of her hand. Inwardly, Lauren smirked.

"And even though Maze did not testify on his own behalf, he stated for the record during his police interrogation that his wife had promised to take her own life that night." A calculated pause. "Did she? How are we to know? Is she alive? How are we to know? Did she swim to shore or was picked up by native fishermen and carried to shore? How are we to know? How are we to know anything?"

Audible murmurs resonated throughout the courtroom. "And furthermore, if she didn't swim, where is the body? The prosecution hasn't produced one because there isn't one. There's no body, no weapon, and no witnesses who came forward to testify that they saw Mr. Maze harm his wife in any way, much less kill her. The smoking gun the prosecution wants you to see doesn't exist. There isn't one. Nothing! As a matter of fact, there is nothing one can logically conclude based upon testimony given and evidence provided. We don't know anything. I don't know, Mr. Maze doesn't know, Mr. Bradley doesn't know, Judge Howell doesn't know, and *none of you know*. Only God Himself knows." Lauren glared sternly at the jury and placed both hands on the barrier separating her from them.

Suddenly, juror number six transformed. Instead of a plump, but otherwise neatly dressed matronly woman, Lauren was staring intently at the all too familiar likeness of the Almighty. He sat quietly looking sternly in her direction.

Startled once more, Lauren gasped, quickly removing her hands from the barrier. It was as if she had touched something contaminated. Taking a few deep, cleansing breaths and one large gulp of water, Lauren grew determined not to let the vision bother her and fight through it.

"So," she continued, "So, what does all of this mean? Putting everything together, the testimony, the flimsy evidence, and shoddy police work? It all culminates in reasonable doubt. Plain and simple. The prosecution would like you to believe it is reasonable to suggest Mr. Maze killed his wife."

Suddenly, Lauren did a double-take. Along with juror six, jurors two and eleven also transformed into God. Lauren was temporarily spooked, but she pressed on.

"What motive does the prosecution offer? A small life insurance policy? Most couples carry them. I'm sure a few of you have policies in place in case of the unexpected and untimely death of your spouse."

Jurors one and seven simultaneously turned into God. Rattled, but not broken, Lauren stumbled on. "The . . . Mr. Bradley . . . the . . . the prosecution . . . " Lauren walked to the defense table, poured herself a third glass of water, and slammed it down like a veteran whiskey drinker. "Sorry, a bit warm in here. At least it is to me." Fighting the urge to run, scream, or both, Lauren continued. "I tell you, the prosecution would like you to believe it's reasonable that Mr. Maze killed his wife, because hey, where else could she be, right? Only that's not the law. That, I remind you, is not the law."

Two more jurors transformed into God and Lauren desperately needed to look away. But no, she had to stay focused on the task at hand. She toughened. She walked up to one of the "Gods" staring at her, glared, and defiantly shook her head at Him. He wasn't going to drive her crazy that easily.

She placed her hands on the wooden bench separating

herself from the Almighty, who was sitting patiently, her hands comfortably rested upon His knees. God smiled back at her. "Go ahead, sit there; stare at me if you must. But hear every word I say and mark them well."

Lauren continued. "Their deduction," she pointed to the prosecution table, "is not, I repeat, NOT within a reasonable conclusion of guilt. It's underwhelming, to say the least, and has so many holes it's far afield from reasonable doubt in a murder case."

In full throttle, Lauren turned her back on the jury as well as, symbolically, on God. She was not about to let anything stand in the way of her performance. She was in her element and determined to shine.

"Ask yourselves this," she continued, selecting her words with care. "Is it reasonable or is it not that a woman suffering terribly from both bipolar and borderline personality disorders, coupled with a sad history of suicidal tendencies, on a night which she and her husband had a deeply emotional argument, might, *just might,* have let her mind go over the edge, sadly causing her to follow through on her earlier threat of personal destruction?" Her voice elevated for effect. "Is that, or is that not equally REASONABLE SPECULATION as to what happened to Amanda Maze that fateful night?"

Distraught and reacting angrily, Amanda's Maze's mother, sitting with her husband in the first row behind Bradley's bench, rose to her feet. She could no longer listen to any more distorted lies against her daughter. She could no longer contain her emotions and felt a strong urge to voice her extreme distaste for this personal and vicious attack on her precious Amanda's character.

Bradley had warned the parents what the defense would likely say against their daughter in the closing arguments and had cautioned them against lashing out in any fashion. Amanda's mother, knowing how difficult it would be for her to remain silent, even thought about staying home. But since her entire world had disappeared along with Amanda under those Pacific waves, she would never have been able to forgive herself if she did. As much as she knew it would hurt, she had been compelled to come to her daughter's defense.

Something was wrong. As she was trying to vocalize her frustration, she found she was having a great deal of difficulty. Her vision blurred. Her legs grew weak. Thought eluded her. She felt herself slipping out of consciousness. The last thing the woman remembered before going limp into her husband's trembling arms was believing she had screamed the word "LIES!" Only no words escaped her lips.

The spectators gasped as Bradley waved for assistance. Two officers helped remove the unconscious woman as Judge Howell banged her gavel in an attempt to restore some semblance of order. Camera bulbs flashed.

"There will be no pictures!" the judge shouted at the press booth.

Slowly, the courtroom quieted.

"You may proceed, Ms. Hill."

Normally, Lauren would have been gloating inwardly. She wouldn't have cared how her callousness had caused loved ones to become distraught. It mattered not. Her job was to defend her client. If the prosecution's side became incensed because of the harshness of her words or tone, all the better. However, as she gazed at Amanda's mother being carried out, Lauren found a moment of compassion. She, too, was a mother. What if it had been her daughter? How well would she have survived such an ordeal? Lowering her voice, Lauren continued.

"Let me be clear, Amanda Maze is not the one on trial here, and I'm not suggesting she deliberately took her own life knowing that her husband would be viciously attacked. Mrs. Maze was a tortured, tormented soul deserving great respect. She was not in complete control of her faculties. But the fact remains, her husband is not a callous killer. He is very much a victim, a widower, the victim of an overzealous prosecution grasping at straws to answer questions by filling gaps with speculation and fabrication, a victim of this day and age of sensational journalism, a victim of fate and circumstance, and ultimately, a victim of his love for a broken woman."

Lauren finally turned back to the jury. All twelve jurors staring back at her were God. Each looking the same, with the same expression—displeased and reproachful.

"Ladies and gentlemen of the jury," she concluded, staring boldly into the eyes of God, "this is the truth I bring before you."

CHAPTER NINETEEN

As the sun sank into the western sky, the darkening shadows cast by downtown skyscrapers grew longer and longer on the bustling streets below. Lauren Hill stood, staring blankly out her corner office window on the twenty-sixth floor, deep in meditative thought. Orange gave way to hues of pinks and purples as she contemplated the day's events, but she didn't particularly notice the beauty of the colors.

Lauren's work was done, the case finished. To be sure, it was not one of her more stellar performances. In fact, she could not remember a time when her execution had been worse in the closing days. She prided herself on perfection. When a perfectly laid plan had come together and she could see the light at the end of a long, dark tunnel that was when Lauren was usually at her best. Not this time. This time, she had barely survived.

On the ground level, streetlights flickered to life, illuminating both highway and sidewalk, one grid at a time. Staring out at the dusky hues of sunset, Lauren continued to reason as the vast urbanity around her lit up.

Lauren tried to process why God was targeting her. *"6:16 . . . 6:16,"* she kept mumbling to herself, over and over: the Seven Deadly Sins God had revealed to her. *What book was that in?* she wondered. With everything going on, she couldn't remember. It was right there on the tip of her tongue. "Damn it!"

Because official courtroom duties had taken precedence over learning and retaining Scripture, Lauren had pushed it aside. Now, when she needed recall, it had escaped her. *That was stupid. Why didn't I write it down?* Lauren felt compelled to read those verses again, to hear the full message meant for her—everything.

Thinking turned to dwelling, dwelling to obsession. Her OCD was kicking in. Lauren knew she would find neither peace nor rest until she fully grasped the meaning of what God was conveying to her, but there wasn't a Bible in her office. Lauren needed a clear head. She knew exactly how to clear it.

Lauren walked to the wet bar in the opposite corner of the room, past a bookcase filled with law books and her professionally framed diploma from UCLA School of Law. Opening the etched glass door, she searched amongst the assorted bottles of bourbon, cognac, and whiskey. None of those would do. She reached in, pulled out a fifth of vodka, and unscrewed the top. She then went to the apartment-sized refrigerator and took out a bottle of tonic water. Setting it on the counter, she reached for a tall glass. Pouring a third of a glass of vodka, she stopped, thought twice, and filled it to about half. "Gonna need something a wee bit stronger," she said aloud.

It was only then that Lauren realized darkness had descended upon her. She flicked on the light and walked back to the window. She sipped. "Yeah, that's it." She sipped again and cocked her head back. Lights in the office directly across the street suddenly came on. Squinting, she could faintly see a human form open the top drawer of a tan filing cabinet. She was noticing details. *Good!* She felt much better.

Off to the northwest, Lauren saw a bright flash of light out of the corner of her eye. Turning, she couldn't see anything, at first. Suddenly, there was another flash. That too was good. A rare thunderstorm was moving in from off the ocean. "Nice. Let it pour."

A thought came to mind. Walking to her desk, she pushed the intercom, hoping more than believing her secretary hadn't gone home for the evening without first telling her. Granted, it was just past five o'clock and Rose was under no moral obligation to stick around, but still. It was just a courtesy her paralegal had afforded her on days juries began deliberating.

Unless pressing duties called for her immediate attention at home, Rose Keller usually continued intercepting incoming calls from both family and the courthouse, while performing various nominal duties and unfinished business. This wasn't all out of the goodness of her heart, though. Rose was much more curious than Lauren to know once a jury had reached a verdict. Of course, there was no way of knowing exactly what the verdict would be, but at least she would be the first to know that a decision had been reached. Based upon the amount of time taken to deliberate, Rose always tried to guess the outcome.

"Rose?"

After an anxious beat, the light came on. "Yes, Ms. Hill."

Relief. "Quick, I need you to read me something."

Rose was devoted to her employer and shone in her position. She was Lauren's Girl Friday, an invaluable, go-to office manager whom Lauren trusted implicitly. She had been making things run smoothly for over eight years. Swift of mind as well as foot, she effortlessly performed her duties, running circles around many in her profession half her age. She had learned shortcuts and worked smarter, not harder. It served her well. She had discovered a long time ago that being a paralegal in LA was a dog-eat-dog world, more like Darwin's survival of the fittest. If she wanted to last long in the business, she knew she had to learn nearly as much about law as Lauren. When Lauren was looking for a paralegal at the time she was starting her own firm, she knew immediately Rose was exactly who she was looking for.

Lauren did not have time for, nor would she ever stand for, someone sitting around, polishing her nails and trying to look pretty for male clientele. Lauren was all business and demanded professionalism on the highest level. Rose was that individual. During her first interview, Lauren had known the caliber of person she was. From that moment on, she much appreciated her hard work, long hours, and tireless dedication. Rose never disappointed.

Although long past the point of dying her graying hair to impress the opposite sex, Rose was still a looker. She may have been past the prime of life, but still, she looked a great deal younger than her sixty-three years. Her makeup was always tasteful, her smile cheerful even on the most trying of days, Rose kept herself fit, and her attire was always business professional. She truly seemed to enjoy coming to work.

"Yes, Ms. Hill, I'll be right in."

"No, no! From there. From your desk." Lauren stopped her, taking a large sip of her drink.

"Whatever you say, Ms. Hill," Rose said cordially. "What would you like read?"

"Scripture."

"Excuse me, Ms. Hill? You mean Bible verse?"

"Yes, pull it up on the computer or something. 6:16."

"6:16, Ms. Hill?" Rose didn't understand much about the Bible, but she knew enough about it to understand her employer was being vague in what she was asking for.

"Yeah, those sin things. The seven deadly ones! Read them for me."

"Yes, Ms. Hill, searching now."

In the background, Lauren could hear Rose's nimble fingers deftly flying across the computer keys. After a brief pause, there was more typing.

"Here you go, Ms. Hill." Rose cleared her throat. "Excuse me. 'There are six things the Lord hates, seven of which are detest—'"

Suddenly, nothing but static.

At first, Lauren thought something was wrong with the receiver. "Hello?" Nothing. Lauren gave the intercom a well-placed smack. "C'mon, stupid thing!"

Then the familiar voice on the other end apologized for the interruption and announced Maze's arrival. Lauren felt stupid for hitting the machine, but at least no one had been around to see it.

Rain pattered against the windows as Lauren fumed. *Why now?* Why did her client have to show up at such an inopportune moment? Maze had said he was only stepping out just long enough to grab a bite to eat; Lauren couldn't help thinking of the Last Supper. She had no idea so much time had elapsed. *Why couldn't God have slowed time now?* she wondered. Lauren needed much more of it to herself.

She sighed. Pressing the "speak" button, she told Rose to "hold the thought," then giving it further thought, informed her to forget she had ever mentioned the reading. "Send him in."

"Right away. You may go . . . "

Lauren pressed a button, and the intercom went dead. She slammed back the rest of her drink as the door opened. Maze entered alone.

"Ms. Hill?" he said, more as a question than a statement. Timidly, he shut the door behind him.

Lauren put on her best fake smile. "How are you feeling, Maze?"

"How should I say it? More hopeful than scared. But scared nonetheless."

"But hopeful, no?"

"Yes. I guess I'm confident enough."

Not particularly interested in his answer either way, Lauren crossed the office toward the wet bar. "What are you drinking?"

"Water."

"Sparkling or flat?"

"Water. Just plain water."

Lauren turned to get him a glass when, suddenly, the door to the office burst open. A soaking wet Ryan Thompson entered. Standing just inside the entrance, he gently shook the rainwater out of his hair and looked up to see his boss lady staring questioningly at him.

"First time, I swear. First time I've ever been caught in the rain without an umbrella. Thought I was going to beat it."

"Well, looks like you were wrong. Now stop shaking like a wet poodle all over my office," Lauren said with a short, sarcastic laugh.

Ryan obeyed and stepped over to shake Maze's hand. He asked how Maze was feeling, although he didn't care in the least how the man felt. It was simply something to say in acknowledgment of Maze's presence.

"Already been established," Lauren stated. More sarcasm. No laughter, this time. "Why don't you fix us some drinks?"

"Great," he said, eagerly rubbing his hands together. "What are you having?"

Simultaneously, Lauren said, "Vodka and tonic," while Maze answered, "Water."

Ryan looked back and forth between the two of them. Lauren motioned with a quick nod toward the bar and Ryan went to work.

Maze walked somberly in the opposite direction to the sofa and sat down, sinking deep into the plush material. Nervously, he began rubbing the arm of it, making random swirls on the two-tone pattern. He noticed that if he stroked in one direction, it was a deep, rich brown. When he stroked in the opposite direction, a golden color appeared.

Lauren watched him with fascination. He seemed innocent,

almost childlike. For the first time, he wasn't acting like the excitable Maze she had seen seated beside her in court. From the time they had first met in her office, she hadn't been able to read him, couldn't tell whether he had committed that awful murder—and honestly didn't care one way or the other. It wasn't her job to care. If she wanted to care, she would have become a doctor. That's what they do, care. Not her.

Why, she wondered, *didn't he behave like this during the trial?* The longer she studied the subdued individual sitting before her, the more she was beginning to believe the spindly Maze was incapable of committing murder.

Distracting her from her observations, Ryan walked back and handed Maze an opened bottle of water, then turned to hand Lauren her deceptive concoction; it looked like water, but it was much dryer. Ryan sat on the sofa next to Maze, while Lauren walked to the window to watch the storm through the wavy rivulets of water streaming down the paned glass. An eerie silence permeated the room. It wasn't a tense standoff type of silence, more a contemplative solemnity. Silence, nonetheless. Lauren relished it.

Maze wanted to talk, needed to voice concerns, only he didn't know how to start. Actually, he felt it out of place to speak. Maze knew that when it came to Lauren, he was a grating irritant, like fingernails scraping across a slate chalkboard. From day one, he had always felt uncomfortable around her. He felt Lauren's piercing eyes upon him whenever he voiced an opinion or nervously fidgeted, as he was doing that moment. But he couldn't help it. He was scared for his life. He looked down at his legs. They were going a mile a minute, bouncing uncontrollably. He squeezed his kneecaps, tight. His legs ceased their involuntary movement. Needing to do anything but watch the clock, he took a sip of water and went back to doodling on the sofa. It was mindless activity, but at least it passed the time.

A low, alcohol-induced hum rang distantly in Lauren's ears. She cleared her mind and just listened. Closing her eyes, she became enraptured by the unwavering reverberations within her inner ear. It was as if a strange force were tugging at her. She felt herself starting to spiral.

"Well, we gave it to the jury." Ryan clapped a hand against his knee.

Both Lauren and Maze were startled back to reality. Lauren turned to face him, but neither one offered acknowledgment. For different reasons, both lawyer and client had an inexplicable feeling of impending doom.

"Well," Ryan continued, "I, for one, feel confident, very confident."

Nervously, Maze inquired, "How long does it usually take?"

Ryan held his hands out from him, palms up. "Varies. You can never know."

"The longer, the better, right? That's what I've heard, the longer, the better."

"I'd say," Ryan offered.

"Is that right, Miss Hill?"

Looking out the window, Lauren emptied her glass in one long, final swig. "A storm is brewin'. A big, ugly storm."

Thunder roared, and lightning flashed, lighting up the evening sky. Maze and Ryan jumped up from their seats. Lauren calmly turned to face them.

"Is that true, Miss Hill? Is it better if they take longer?" Maze stammered.

Lauren studied Maze. Something about him seemed to have changed in the last few minutes, but she couldn't put her finger on it. He just didn't seem the same as when he was aimlessly finger-doodling in the pattern on her sofa. Maze lifted his gaze toward her. Yes, she was sure there was something: a flood of despair behind a crumbling dam, a distant rage welling up inside, perhaps.

Lauren wasn't sure which it was. All she knew was anxiety was brewing inside her. She would never want to be alone with him; that was certain.

Unflinchingly, Lauren countered with her own question. "You been following your doctor's instructions?"

"I promised you I would," he said with a touch of repressed hostility. "But I figured this afternoon, now that the trial is over, that my own decisions should be good enough. I've found something in God, Miss Hill, something that feels more stabilizing than what's in those pills."

"Something on your mind, Maze? Something you wanna say?" she asked. Lauren saw some ugliness inside him, and she wanted nothing more than to have him spew that ugliness toward her.

However, Maze was a trifle smarter than that. It was the main reason why he had chosen to have water instead of alcohol. He wanted to remain in complete control of his faculties. He didn't want to say or do anything he would later regret. Maze took a long gulp of water. It did nothing to calm his nerves, but it gave him enough time to pull himself back in check. "No. Just asking about the average."

Lauren continued to study her client: his movements, his mannerisms. She purposely left Maze's question unanswered. She could see his frustration building. Maze was on the verge of unraveling and possibly within a fraction of blurting something, something big, something life-altering. If she could just work him a few more minutes, she was sure she could make this happen.

"I'd say it's true," Ryan blundered in. "They take the first vote. That takes but a few minutes. If it isn't unanimous, they go and talk, and talk, and talk some more, until they either vote the same or can't talk anymore. The longer they talk, the more likely they can't vote the same."

Damn, she thought, shooting Ryan a look. *I almost had him.*

Even though Maze hadn't had a drop of alcohol, the fermented distillation known to lawyers the world over as truth serum, Lauren knew without a doubt he was on the verge of spilling his guts. Just at that moment, however, Maze's countenance changed abruptly. Lauren could see the moment had slipped from her grasp.

"But I don't want a hung jury!" Maze snapped. "I want them to all vote the same—not guilty. A hung jury, they'll just try me again. They'll just try me all over again. I can't go through this anymore." Maze bowed his head in his hands, then pounded his fists against his forehead.

Exasperated, Lauren jumped in. "They're gonna vote the same."

"Yeah? How?" Maze was barely able to keep his rage in check.

"Not guilty, Maze," Lauren assured him.

Hearing those beautiful words from her did reassure him, in a sense. Still, there was something he wanted to get off his chest, and Lauren knew it. She waited in cool anticipation. Maze looked at Lauren and the two locked horns until Maze could no longer hold it in.

"I heard Amanda's family—" Then he switched his direction. "Growing up, I ended up going to three different high schools. I used to play baseball. We didn't move or anything, just incidents, always incidents that used to follow me. And hearing them, seeing them. They used to be my family, you know, like looking at old teammates across the field. Conflict in your heart, but I heard them talking about me."

Lauren was a bit confused. Maze was rambling, not making any sense: first talking about different schools, then playing ball, then people following him. He was hopping around too much. Still, she produced a kindly smile, sat back in her chair, and calmly folded her dainty hands over her knee.

Maze looked down at his own hands and continued. "I don't know if you noticed, but I couldn't look at them throughout the trial. Looking at the judge, the jury, those lawyers was enough.

More than I could handle. I couldn't look at them, too. But I heard them whispering between sobs and tears, saying Amanda should never have married me because I'd already been divorced twice. And, and they'd murmur about trust, that you can't trust a man with a background like mine. But that's not true, I'm telling you. It just isn't true." He pounded a clenched fist on his leg.

Lauren was taken aback. It was a hard blow. She was worried Maze had punched himself hard enough to cause injury. But Maze never missed a beat. Even without having a stiff drink, he kept talking.

"The truth is, the first time I married young. Real young. I was eighteen and in the service. Our little boy was born premature, and he died in her arms. From then on, I swear she didn't love me anymore. Like she couldn't. She just couldn't."

The longer Maze talked, the more distraught he became. Tears welled in the corner of his eyes as he revealed his painful relationship history. At least, for Lauren, it was painful to listen to and not in a compassionate way. She was hoping that all of this was leading somewhere, possibly to a confession of some sort.

"Then when I was twenty-five, yeah, I admit we beat each other up a few times. Didn't know no other way. It wasn't meant to be, me and her. She always taunted, and I was always angry." Maze looked up at Lauren. "I loved my wife. You know that, right? I loved her like I never loved anyone."

Lauren was surprised. She could sense imminent collapse. Leaning back so Maze could not see him, Ryan circled the air with his finger near his left ear to sign *crazy*. Lauren nodded slightly in acknowledgment and looked at Maze.

Anxiety building, he stood. "I was never religious . . . never. I was the kid that used to hurt things—bugs, small animals—cut them up." Maze's voice seemed to elevate with excitement. "But then, I got older and stopped hurting them and believing in my own powers. I started finding ways to justify that what I was doing was okay. If I stole something, it was because it shouldn'ta been withheld from me in the first place. If I hurt something or someone, well I figured they deserved it."

Lauren locked eyes carefully with Ryan. She nodded purposefully in agreement that Maze was not all there. Lauren saw the gleam in Maze's eye. He seemed almost to enjoy reliving his past destructive behavior.

"And they probably did, right?"

Lauren only nodded in false agreement.

"But I didn't have no God," Maze continued. "My parents hated religion. They were social climbers, used to mock religion. They said it was only for the weak-minded, like superstitions, but organized into well-funded machines. What did talking to God or about God ever do for anyone, anyway?" Maze glanced at both Ryan and Lauren. "Right? Right? Just talkin' 'bout a higher power no one had ever seen. As I got older, I didn't see the point, either. It didn't make any sense to me that all the power in life was not in your own hands. If one's life was a car, weren't they also the driver? But I see something I never did before. I see order. I see the kind of order in God that clearly is. I don't know. I can't explain it, don't know the words, I guess. But I find comfort in knowing I'm not alone, anymore. I know there's a God."

Maze looked down at his hands, studying them. His tone lowered to nearly a whisper. "I never felt so alone with just my hands, like I have."

Clearly, Maze was ridden with guilt. Lauren crossed to him, taking his hands in hers. Touched, Maze looked up at her. It was the most warmth she had ever shown to him.

"I don't have anywhere to go. There's no grave, no way to show remorse." He looked into Lauren's eyes. "They think I did it, too. They believed me at first, but now, now her whole family thinks I loved her. Now, I'm not only alone; I feel abandoned."

Lauren stepped away, feeling powerless. Maybe, like everyone else in his life, she had misjudged him. He did have a history of killing animals in gruesome ways she found disturbing, but that proved nothing. It didn't make him a killer. She, too, had been misunderstood the past couple of days. She wasn't crazy, either. She had seen God.

"I know there's nothin' more you can do. You've done everything you could. And I thank you. I thank you for it," Maze offered.

Ryan crossed the room and pulled a black umbrella out of the can. "Hey, remember, she's never lost a case. We've never lost a case." Then he turned to Lauren, holding up her umbrella. "Mind if I borrow this?"

"Yeah," Maze interjected. "But there's a first time for everything."

Lauren looked at Ryan. "Take Maze back to his hotel room." Then she ordered Maze, "Go get some sleep, and take your medication."

"I can't get the regret out of my mind."

"Dose up."

"I threw them away when the jury took the case. Maybe I shouldn't have yelled at her, Miss Hill," Maze babbled on. "Maybe I should have controlled myself more. Maybe I should have stayed with her all night instead of leaving her alone."

"Hey," Ryan said, taking Maze by the arm. "You had a marital argument, a natural dispute. Everyone does. You're making yourself out to be responsible for something beyond your control."

"But I'm the one condemned."

As Lauren watched the two of them head for the exit, she pondered Maze's last statement. He wasn't condemned, at least not by a jury. They were still in deliberation. Or was there something more to it than that? She didn't know. In thoughtful silence, Lauren walked back to her desk.

CHAPTER TWENTY

Lightning flashed, and the thunder rolled over the darkening, purple heavens above the Hill homestead. The air was thick, saturated with an uncharacteristic humidity, even as the wind picked up. Soon, the fast-moving cold front was howling in the normally quiet, upscale community. Constance could hear the branches from the ripening lemon tree in the front yard as they scraped across the picture window of the living room. Thick drops smacked loudly against the hard surfaces outside. Soon, water ran in rivulets toward low areas. The torrent roared over the parched earth, unable to soak in. Lightning flashed, again. The lights flickered. Lost in her own world, Constance barely noticed.

Then, suddenly, the raging tempest went from a steady downpour to an almost nonexistent, mild drizzle. The wind died down to a peaceful quiet. As quickly as it came, the storm rapidly moved off toward the eastern mountains and beyond. Once over the arid desert, the clouds dissipated. It rarely rained in Los Angeles and more rarely still in the California desert.

Deep in thought in the dining area of the spacious, raised ranch, Constance was randomly sliding a stainless-steel fork across her plate. She picked at her chicken. It looked as if she were playing a weird game of keep-away from the broccoli spears. At first, Dennis watched her in amusement. He knew his daughter honestly did not care for green vegetables unless they were coated with a thick, hearty layer of melted cheddar. Since he was the chef that evening, as he was most every evening, that was not going to happen. Constance was going to have to do without. Wolfgang Puck, he was not.

The longer he watched, however, the more he realized Constance wasn't picking because she didn't like what had been placed in front of her, but rather because she was lost in a world of her own creation. What world that was, he had no earthly idea, but he had a pretty good idea his daughter wasn't having pleasant thoughts. Dennis cleared his plate and began speaking from the sink. Constance didn't hear a word her father said.

Dennis shook his head and turned on the hot water. He squirted a generous amount of dish soap into the steady stream. Suds thickened and rose up from the water. Dennis hardly ever ran the dishwasher. He felt it was more work loading and unloading it than if he simply washed them by hand. Dennis placed the dishes in the sink, glancing at his daughter between each item placed on the draining board. Through it all, Constance never moved. He turned off the water and stepped away from the domestic duties he had grown more accustomed to since Lauren started her own practice eight years ago. As his wife had spent longer and longer periods of time at the office and wherever else entailed playing lawyer, Dennis' chores had steadily increased. Lauren rather unlovingly left notes for him, to-do lists of what she expected to have accomplished by the time she walked through the door after an exceedingly long, tedious day. It surely wasn't how he had envisioned his life, the embarrassing role reversal, but someone had to take care of their child.

Dennis hated his lot in life, but after his meeting with his publisher earlier in the day, he felt he might have finally crested that long hill to see something better on the other side. Setting the dish towel on the counter, he walked to the table, pulled up a chair next to his teenage girl, and patiently waited.

After a few moments, Constance finally realized her father was there, and she asked if he had said something. Forgetting what it was about schoolwork he had wanted to ask her, Dennis shrugged. It wasn't that important. What seemed to be bothering his daughter was. "Doesn't matter. What's on your mind?"

"Think I wanna go see Mom."

Dennis wasn't expecting it. He thought maybe she had a problem in school or an argument with her best friend. Not that. Dennis looked up at the clock. *5:22.* "You mean now?"

"Right now."

Surprised at the urgency in her voice, Dennis stared blankly at his daughter.

"She's not still in court at this hour, is she?"

"No, I don't believe so. I heard on the radio, earlier, they handed the case over to the jury, so I assume—"

Constance bolted out of her chair and grabbed a sweater out of the closet. She was even more determined to find out what her mother was up to. Still rather sticky outside, it was much too warm for a raincoat. She only needed something to provide a scant amount of protection from the light drizzle.

Dennis put up mild resistance. "I don't know. By the time we get downtown, it will be close to half past six."

"So?"

"So it's likely your mother will be on her way home by then and we'll pass her on the freeway without ever seeing her. Besides, it's a school night."

Constance folded her arms across her chest, annoyed. She tapped her foot on the hardwood floor. Relenting, Dennis pushed away from the table and stood up. Holding his hands up in surrender, he said, "Okay, I guess we can go. But first, text her and see if she's free."

"Mom's never free."

Dennis hoped his daughter was just referring to time and not thinking of other, less becoming meanings. Either way, he couldn't argue with Constance: Lauren rarely answered his texts. "Well, at least try."

Constance grabbed her phone off the table, and soon her thumbs were flying on her iPhone. Dennis got the set of keys off the counter, and the two of them headed out the door. Surprisingly, the temperature had dropped noticeably since the massive cold front had moved through. That was rarely the case. But it felt good. The two of them opened their doors, slid in, and buckled their seat belts. Dennis then started the car.

"So, is your mom available?"

"I don't know. She hasn't replied."

"She's likely busy. Maybe we shouldn't go. We'll see her later tonight," he said, turning the car off.

"No. I wanna go see her. Please. She's probably still working at the office."

Dennis thought for a moment. *What's with the women I live with?* he wondered. *Both are so demanding. It must be in the genes; at least this one says please.* Before he even finished his thought, Dennis knew he would give in. In reality, he was just as curious to see what his wife was up to. It wasn't unheard of for her to come home late on deliberation days, but it was only in recent months that he questioned Lauren's whereabouts during the day.

CHAPTER TWENTY-ONE

R yan asked Maze to wait outside of Lauren's office. The young attorney wanted a few minutes alone with his boss. Maze glanced at Lauren, and she nodded approval for him to leave.

"Weird, but he feels responsible, somehow," Ryan said.

"I suppose."

Just then, a meek knock sounded at the door. It was Rose. "It's only me, Ms. Hill. Sorry to bother you, but I have the court transcripts you asked for."

"That's okay, Rose."

The secretary hastily placed the files on her desk. "Also, I printed what you asked me to read earlier. It's clipped on top."

Nonchalantly, Lauren walked to her desk and picked up the files Rose had left. Removing the paperclip, she immediately became transfixed by Proverbs and only faintly heard Ryan speak. Finally tearing herself away from Scripture, she asked him to repeat his response.

"You're obviously distracted. I said I've been seeing them for weeks straight," he repeated.

"Yeah, but did you get a good look at them today?"

"Yeah, I saw them. What are you reading, by the way?"

"Nothing," she snapped, curtly. "What did they look like?" Lauren was determined not to stray off subject.

"The jurors? Like damn jurors."

"Nothing unusual, then?" Lauren eyed him.

"I don't know what it is you think I didn't see, but I certainly saw them, and then we basically said, 'Here ya go, another man's fate. You be the final arbitrators.' I have to admit though, this is my favorite part, sitting back and waiting for the phone to ring."

"You'd rather wait for the bell than finish the fight?"

"I didn't say that."

"Because you do tend to be on the lazy side."

"I do not," he snapped, surprised at Lauren's tone. Then, changing his own, "I submit I'm actually overworked and underpaid."

Lauren smirked. "Uh huh. That's the way it should be. It's the difference between the eagle and the dodo."

"Really," Ryan smiled. "How's that?"

"Hunger makes you lean, smart, and mean. Satiation, on the other hand, leaves you fat, feeble, and fed on."

"Gawd, I'll have to ask Constance the next time I see her. You must be a barrel of laughs at home."

Lauren's cell phone buzzed with a text from Bradley.

One last quickie?

Sure, she thumbed her reply.

Looking up at Ryan, "You leave my daughter out of this. I laugh as much as anyone else when something is funny. Murder trials aren't humorous."

Hotel? Bradley's text read.

"Okay, okay. Touché." Ryan said dejectedly.

My office, she texted.

"But don't you ever let up, Lauren?" Ryan continued. "Don't

you at least like to bask in the fact that the work is done? Now we just sit back and wait," he said, folding his hands behind his head for emphasis.

See u in 20.

"Who keeps texting you?" Ryan asked.

"Oh, nobody."

"Nobody?"

Lauren played it cool. "So, where were we?"

BZZzzzz!

Lauren didn't read the text but held it up without reading it to show Ryan. "See, nobody," she said, flipping it into the top desk drawer. "Oh yes, I remember. You were about to attempt to explicate the virtues of chance over the vice of control."

"Cute."

"Oh, enough of this. Take Maze back to the hotel and stay with him. Don't let him do anything stupid."

"Why? What is it you think he's gonna do?"

"I don't really know, but once again, I'll take control over chance any day."

"I should have seen that coming." Picking up the umbrella, he repeated, "You don't mind if I use this?"

"Take it," she said, with a wave of the hand. "Just bring it back." Lauren watched him gather himself together. Then, as an afterthought, she said, "He's obsessive, you know."

"Think it's just the stress, or something more?"

"He's a manic depressive."

Ryan took his hand off the doorknob and turned. "What?"

"Yeah. Cyclothymia."

Ryan had never heard of the condition. He held out his hands at a loss and stared blankly at his employer.

"I had him diagnosed. Just trying to cover all bases."

"What is it?"

"A form of mania, but milder."

"You mean something similar to what his wife had?"

Lauren nodded. "That's why the police had been called to their house so often," Lauren laughed. "I fucked Bradley."

"You mean with discovery."

"No, literally." Lauren interrupted. "I fucked him a few times during the trial."

"What? Wait . . . What?" Ryan studied her to see if she was pulling his leg.

"Other than the buzz I currently have, it's the best way I know to take the edge off." Lauren winked. The vodka was working brilliantly. She was feeling no pain.

Truth serum. "Oh, shit," he thought, "she isn't kidding." Ryan was dumbfounded. He stood there stammering for a moment. Unethical, hell, her decision was potentially career-ending, for her and the prosecutor. However, this was his boss.

Knowing too much in certain circles could get one killed. Ryan didn't feel he had anything to worry about in that regard. He didn't believe Lauren was capable of doing what Maze did (Ryan now thought Maze was just as guilty as Charles Manson, John Wayne Gacy, or that pretty boy, Ted Bundy). But what the hell was he going to do with this disclosure?

In the end, there was nothing he could do or at least was willing to do. He hadn't asked to be privy to such private and certainly damaging information. Ryan decided to forget she ever told him. The less he could recall, the better.

But Bradley? Him? He nearly laughed. *Never in a million years would I have guessed that.*

Lauren knew better than to place herself in such a hazardous position. That, too, was not like her. All humor aside, he raised a hand to his forehead.

"I know nothing, but with the prosecutor? C'mon, Lauren! It's the best way I know to get disbarred!"

"You know what they say," Lauren grinned. "Keep your

friends close and your enemies—"

"I know, I know . . . closer."

"No. By the balls." She gestured palm up, fingers spread wide and pointing upward.

Ryan couldn't control himself. He burst into nervous laughter. Still, he was uncomfortable with the knowledge he now possessed. He only hoped Lauren knew what she was doing and was not getting herself into a hole she could not possibly crawl out of.

"Sex softens a man's mind. God bless his wife. She must be bored out of her fuckin' mind. He fucks as mechanically as he did when I worked in the DA's office."

Still laughing nervously, Ryan said, "No more, I can't take anymore," Ryan held up a hand as if warding off evil spirits. "Way too much information. Now, I'm probably under some ethical duty I intend to shirk." Then, as an afterthought, he added, "Wait, what about—" He poked a thumb toward the door.

"Maze? Hell no, I wouldn't fuck him! I'm not a whore!"

"No, not that! What we were talking about, before. Did Bradley know Maze was unhinged?"

"Nah," she said, swatting at the air as if there was a bug. "He never thought to check."

"But you never disclosed that?"

"Look," she said, getting down to business. "We don't know that it's relevant. The police did their investigation; the cruise line did theirs. Nobody bothered to pursue that possibility."

"You're fuckin' joking, right?" Ryan interrupted.

Lauren folded her arms across her chest.

"Wait, does Maze know any of this?"

"No," Lauren said, seriously annoyed. "It's something I saw in him."

"Saw? Saw what? I don't see anything."

"Just something," she said, reflectively. "What was it exactly did I see? Oh, yes." Snapping out of it, she continued. "Look,

I don't want to go into specific details, but I've seen it before. Classic symptoms. Anyway, I took him to a doctor. He had been up and down: peaks were high, his lows extremely low. Doctors adjusted his medication, trying to find the right balance so there was a consistency between the previous dose and when the next one kicked in. They obviously didn't get it right. His mind kept going into overdrive."

Ryan shuffled nervously.

"Look, this is all about presentation, Ryan. You have to put them in the best possible light. We doll these jokers up—nice suit, tie, haircut, the works, right?"

Ryan nodded.

"But we don't just stop there, with the outside," Lauren continued. "We clean up their act on the inside, too. This is war, remember."

Ryan understood. He was truly beginning to see the ins and outs, those things that were not taught in the classroom. He was young, but far from stupid. "I get it, Lauren, but can you tell me something? What was all that about in court? The running out? And why take the Bible off the bench?"

Coolly, Lauren looked up at Ryan. "I thought I saw God."

"Huh?"

"I honestly thought I saw Judge Howell morph into God."

As much as he wanted to believe Lauren was playing another game with him, Ryan saw by her stone-faced expression that she might be serious. His initial reaction was to think that she, like her client, was losing touch with reality. That would explain the Bradley thing. Only, the more he looked upon her, the more that seemed unlikely. She appeared, as always, to be perfectly in control.

"You're not following me? I thought I saw God. He was talking to me, just as we are, now."

Seeing God was one thing. It could be chalked up to any

number of things. But conversing with him was something on a different plane.

"You're kidding me, right?"

Lauren knew it was probably a bad mistake to let Ryan in on what had been taking place, that she should have just made something up. She only told him because she knew he would keep his mouth shut about it, at least for the time being, anyway. She wanted to tell someone, and he seemed the safest person. However, if this was his reaction, she could see it was an error. She applied her brand of damage control.

"Yeah, of course! Just playing with you."

"Okay, you got me. So, then why did you take it?"

"I don't honestly know my motivation, at the time. I just felt I had to look something up quickly."

"So, you've never opened a Bible in your life? That you just had to bolt to the bench and swipe."

"I'll have you know I went to Sunday school until the age of twelve."

"Really? So, what happened after twelve? Why suddenly stop going? Sex took the edge off more than faith?"

Lauren was taken aback. Arms folded, she replied, "Ha-ha . . . ass."

"No, really, why did you stop going?"

"I guess I just grew out of it. I wanted something more, something more than studying miracles and praising God. Religion seemed so empty."

"What more did you need?"

"My own signs and wonders."

Ryan didn't know where else to go with this. It was the strangest conversation he had ever had, full of bizarre twists, and he was uncomfortable. He needed to get out of there and had the perfect out. "I better go . . . take him back to the hotel," Ryan pointed to the door, meaning Maze. "Before he blows a gasket."

CHAPTER TWENTY-TWO

Alone at her desk, Lauren looked down at her watch, tossed the court transcripts indifferently aside, and began reading Proverbs. As she perused, she got it. Certainly, some of the *sins* did apply to her—but not all of them. "Gluttony. Seriously?" She looked down at her slim figure and laughed aloud. And what about "sloth?" Unlike Maze or Ryan, she was far from lazy. She could be accused of being overzealous, but Lauren prided herself on being tireless. In her profession, she couldn't afford to be a slacker. One did not become as in demand or wealthy as she had, by taking it easy.

So, then, if not all the sins applied to her, why was God targeting her? Surely, there were others—drug addicts, murderers, rapists, and other vermin—more deserving of chastening than she. *Why me?*

A knock on her office door. Lauren looked down at her watch. It was too soon for it to be Bradley.

"Rose?" she said, elevating her voice. "What is it? Oh, just come in," she said, continuing to concentrate on the verses in front of her. She barely heard the door open and close.

After a moment of not hearing a sound, she slowly took her eyes off the page and looked up. God was standing in front of her, dapper in a three-piece suit which would make every top designer in the world beg for the secret. Lauren gasped.

"May I sit?" God gestured to the sofa.

The inconvenient timing of The Lord's appearance. *Maybe Bradley will get here early and see what I'm seeing,* she thought. *Somehow, I doubt it.*

Lauren stood with more confidence and gestured for God to relax. God moved over to the sofa and sat down, casually crossing his legs.

"Once again, you picked a fine time to reveal yourself to me."

"Do I detect a note of sarcasm? You're not afraid, now?"

"I wasn't before."

"Ah. I see. Are you sure you are not hallucinating?"

"Don't know if I can be sure of anything, but you said I was not."

"Correct. You are not hallucinating. What you are seeing is real." He glanced at her desk. "I see you are reading what I wrote for you."

"For me?"

"And others, but certainly for you."

"Then yes. Yes, I am."

God smiled, seemingly pleased that some progress had been made.

"So, why are you here?"

Replacing the smile with a stern countenance, God glared at Lauren. "Because our exchange is incomplete."

"I've read. I know each of the deadly sins," she said, speedily beginning to rattle them off.

"Ah, yes, yes," he interrupted, "But that is what you compartmentalized in your mind, memorization for mere reference. But do you know them here in your heart?" God said, tapping His chest with an index finger.

Lauren shrugged. "What's the difference?"

"Why, the same difference as that between a tick of time and timelessness."

"I don't understand!" Lauren said, throwing up her arms. "What is it you want from me?"

"Nothing."

"Nothing? If it were nothing, you wouldn't be wasting your time. Why are you targeting me?"

"You question My wisdom, Lauren?"

Lauren folded her arms across her chest.

God chuckled. "Because I am God."

"Well then, don't you have better things to do, bigger fish to fry?"

"Than look after you?" God interrupted.

"I don't need looking after. I've done fine on my own. I take perfectly good care of myself, thank you. Always have."

"Aren't you the least bit curious, Lauren, why the Seven Deadly Sins are called the Seven Deadly Sins?"

Lauren paced in front of her desk for a moment. She *was* curious but tried not to show it. Instead, she walked around her desk and shut off her computer. God patiently waited. He brushed away a speck of lint that had attached itself to His jacket sleeve. Unsure how to handle God this time, Lauren went for broke. She turned to face Him. Swallowing hard, she awaited His divine explanation.

Seeing Lauren was finally attentive and receptive to His words, God began.

"Not to worry. I'm not going to give you an answer steeped in ritual and religion. I am going to speak to you as clearly as you might understand, without dogma, articles of faith, or your unwarranted filters of confusion."

Lauren nodded.

"Lauren, your first question is 'Why me?' Is it not?"

A slighter, less confident nod in acknowledgment.

"There are billions upon billions of souls on earth today. Over seven billion of them, to be more exact. Yet it appears to you that I am before you in a special case, as though I am nowhere else in the universe and My time is exclusively for your attention."

Lauren's eyes widened.

"Behold, for I am. Love me, but do not try to understand me. I cannot be grasped by logic or simple, human workings. Be not confused nor attached to the form I've chosen in which our communication takes. It is the communication that is of infinite value. It is the communication which is the light of love." He smiled. "I am talking with you in the form you can understand so that I may have your undivided attention at this critical juncture in your life as you know it. What, then is your life for? What is it for, Lauren?"

A moment earlier, and all the previous moments of her adult life, Lauren had known exactly the purpose of her existence. Now, after just a few sentences from the Almighty, she had no idea.

"I don't know," she said, lowering her head in shame.

"This is not a game of rhetorical questions, Lauren, yet a question for you, nevertheless. I cannot answer it for you. The answer you give is of your own free will. Look at me, Lauren."

Lauren raised her head and opened her eyes to the Almighty God. She was sure He could see her very soul.

"What is your life for, Lauren?"

Lauren didn't know how to respond, wasn't sure she even wanted to make an attempt. After a moment, she realized she had nothing to offer. Slowly and mindlessly, she crossed to the bar. God watched her every step, without judgment.

"Speak honestly. Speak from the heart, Lauren."

"The heart? You want me to speak from the heart?"

"That's the general idea. But not for Me."

"Yeah, well, what if I cut Your tongue in half and then told you to speak from the mouth," she said, angrily. "The heart? You shouldn't ask me such things. You are God. You should already know about my heart and know not to ask me these things."

Lauren was trying to pour herself a drink, but her rage was not allowing her to get it right. She missed her glass and spilled much of the vodka she was pouring.

"What do you want me to do, go through the entire Book of Proverbs and repent my sins?" Lauren was panting with fury. "What are you gonna do now? What awful punishment are you going to threaten me with? You gonna strike me down, shoot a bolt of lightning through my skull? Piss off!"

God rose from the sofa.

"It's my life, mine! and my life is my own business." Lauren paused to breathe. "That's free will."

Before God had brazenly interrupted her life, Lauren had believed she did know what her life was for. She made a great living, provided for an ungrateful family, was the mother of a brat-child, the wife of an unproductive pansy. She worked. That's what she did. Now, when God asked the question of her, she had no clue because she was certain He wanted something more meaningful.

Lauren finished making her drink as well as a mess. She took a long swig and arrogantly turned toward Him. "You wanna drink, or something? You want a drink, God?" she asked, mockingly.

Sadly, yet sternly, God stared into Lauren's eyes. As heated and defiant as ever, she glared back at Him, chest heaving in animated breaths.

"Yeah, the Seven Deadly Sins!" she continued. "Maybe I engage in every single one of them, all the time. Maybe that's the absolute best part of having free will." Lauren sipped. "Tell me, though, what am I missing? Now, there's a question for the Almighty! What am I missing?"

God stood. He knew there was no getting through. He adjusted his suit and started walking toward the exit, neither one of them taking their eyes off one another for a second. Almost to the door, He stopped. He turned one last time to appeal to Lauren's good senses. His gaze was soft, longing, pleading.

"I have but one last question for you. Would you rather have the problem or the answer?"

God turned toward the door and, immediately without touching it, the doorknob turned, and the thick, oak panel slowly swung open. Quietly, He exited.

Lauren sat at her desk, confounded by a stew of rage and confusion. She felt violated by God's repeated, reckless intrusion of her personal space. It was unwarranted and unwelcome. Lauren hadn't asked for His help and certainly didn't pray for guidance or divine intervention in her life. She was doing perfectly fine without God or government judging her. Bad enough she was in the law profession. But for all its flaws, all its imperfections, impropriety, and backroom deals, the law left her alone. God, on the other hand, had chosen to barge in and turn her entire world inside out.

As Lauren stood, picturing herself as some medical anomaly, a grotesque polydactyl being sprouting arm after arm, she counted yet another emotion.

Upon yet another hand, Lauren felt depressed. A crashing wave of melancholia washed over her. Certainly, the infidelity was wrong. She knew she was willfully sinning, at least in God's eyes, and felt a hint of remorse, but she was not particularly motivated to address her emotions. Lauren had tried to separate her personal life from her professional life, rarely succeeding. Lauren played hard with her career, sacrificing those who cared about her most. And now she was paying the price.

As she thought about it, she wasn't sure she wanted to adjust her mindset or cease her extracurricular activities. She *was* doing perfectly fine on her own. Good, bad, or indifferent, Lauren liked the woman she had become and couldn't care less whether or not others liked her: not her family, not her peers, not God Himself. She was who she was, a self-made individual, a raging bitch in a satin skirt and high heels. Let God pick on another, less fortunate soul.

Lauren was successful because she was tough, relentless because she simply had to be. Essentially, there was no other way, not if one wanted to flourish in the business as much as she did. Sure, she was not without flaws. Then again, who was? She had made a few mistakes, but fortunately, they were small and inconsequential, not hindering her career. And even those mistakes had happened because she had let her guard down. It didn't pay to be nice or play fair.

In her defense, however, she also had made plenty of sacrifices: sacrifices her family took for granted. Outside pressures upon her were tremendous. Couldn't they see that? She had a teenage daughter who was borderline rebellious, or at the very least, unappreciative, and don't get her started on her delusional husband. It frustrated her to know Dennis was content playing Mr. Mom and staring blankly for hours at the computer screen. Was he hoping a bestselling novel would miraculously write itself? "Fucking spare me," she fumed.

The longer she counted, the more she seethed. Sure, it was highly unproductive and getting her nowhere, but that was the point God had brought her to. She hadn't been this pent-up with white-hot anger in many months. God had no right to encroach on her life and gum up the works. Her life was not perfect. She was willing to admit that. But it was as close to perfection as it was likely ever going to get. And to be honest, she believed it was a fairly good one, better than what most had. High-end home, high-end vehicles, high-end lifestyle. It was all she needed, and it was all she was ever going to need. How dare He disturb her.

CHAPTER TWENTY-THREE

Seconds after God left, there was a knock on the door.

"It's me, Ms. Hill. I tried to ring, but you didn't pick up. Prosecuting attorney Dillon Bradley is here to see you?"

Sounding only slightly less sarcastic, Lauren said, "Oh, right. Send him in."

The door shut and opened again rather quickly. Dillon Bradley entered eagerly, a spring in his step.

All her frustrations and all her emotions burst out of her in a frenzy of what Dillon took to be passion. Before he was even able to remove his suit jacket, Lauren thrust herself upon him, kissing him hungrily. This was solely about power. Lauren was determined to show God just who was in control of her life.

Lauren hastily unbuttoned Dillon's jacket, pulled it inside out, and threw it toward the coat hooks, missing all of them by a wide margin. Soon, discarded apparel and equipment were strewed over a good portion of the office. Naked, Lauren pushed Bradley onto the desk and aggressively climbed on top of him.

"Yes. Fuck me!" Lauren growled.

Then, between heavy, labored breaths, Bradley revealed, "Want you . . . to know . . . I'm getting a divorce."

Lauren continued to grind and undulate her hips in ever-increasing circular motions over him.

"It's not . . . about this," Bradley continued. "Not because of us."

Uninterested in his empty promises, Lauren increased her intensity, thrusting harder and harder upon him. Lauren rode him, sucking in air and hissing under her breath. "I'm coming."

"Wait! Let's come together." He panted.

One more thrust. "I'm coming."

"This doesn't have to stop between us."

For Lauren, it wasn't about feelings of love. She had never had them, at least not for Bradley. It was simply a lustful act of control. Nothing more. Lauren didn't wait, but came without him, jumped off him as if the amusement ride had come to a complete stop, leaving Dillon unfulfilled. She immediately began dressing and straightening her office.

Just a few blocks away, Constance stared out the passenger window, biting her fingernails as her father drove.

"Traffic's not that bad, tonight," Dennis said. "Almost there."

Constance nodded, but continued staring out the passenger window, wondering what her mother was up to. She suspected the worst. The entire way, she spoke not word one. The two marched into the office building and immediately into the elevator.

The bell dinged, and the doors opened. The two got on the elevator in silence.

Lauren was almost fully dressed when she threw Dillon's pants at him. He felt the need to say something to validate their relationship, to somehow consolidate a connection, but wisely resigned just to put his pants on. Mechanically, Lauren put the items back on her desk in their proper place. In a few minutes, she and her office were neat and tidy. That is, except for Bradley.

He was still buttoning his shirt.

The elevator dinged, and the door opened. Constance, practically lunging out of the confined space, bolted down the hallway toward her mother's office. Dennis was not that eager to see Lauren and lagged behind. Without waiting for him, she flung the door open and entered.

Startled, Rose looked up from her desk. "Oh my, look who's here."

"Is my mom here?" Constance said.

"Why, yes. Yes, she is."

"Can we go in?" Dennis asked, having caught up with his willful child.

"The prosecuting attorney from the trial, Mr. Bradley, is in with her, now."

"I thought the trial was over and they gave the case to the jury," Constance said.

"They did. It's a bit unusual, but not that uncommon he'd be here. Let me give her a buzz."

"No! I want to surprise her," she said, briskly walking toward the door.

"Constance, this is your mother's—"

Constance wasn't hearing any of it and barged in.

"Constance!" Dennis called after her.

The door flew open, and Lauren shot a brief look of displeasure across the room, ready to pounce on the untimely infringement of privacy. Rose knew never to enter unsummoned. At the sight of Constance, Lauren, unlike Dillon, remained composed and never showed a fraction of dismay. She was casually standing at the wet bar, fixing herself a drink. Dillon, on the other hand, was standing slightly turned by Lauren's desk, adjusting his tie. Embarrassed, he was at a loss for words. Immediately suspicious, Constance scanned the room, searching for the smoking gun she was sure she was going to find.

"What are you doing here?" Lauren said, taking the intrusion in stride.

Rushing his efforts, Bradley stammered, "Ah, well, ah, I think that about wraps things up, Lauren."

Constance glanced between Dillon and her mother, while Dennis and Rose rushed in after her.

"I'm sorry, Ms. Hill," Rose said, sheepishly.

"Honey," Dennis began.

Lauren held up a hand as if to say, *Not another word.* Dennis went instantly quiet.

Rose and Dennis were oblivious to the extracurricular activity which had taken place. The office was arranged just as it always had been, immaculate and uncluttered. But Constance was sharp. She knew what she was looking for and spotted it, immediately—a small, foil wrapper sitting crumpled on her mother's desk. It was an uncharacteristic and careless oversight on Lauren's part, but Constance swiftly maneuvered to cover it up.

At the time, Constance had no idea what she was going to do with it. Should she use it as a tool with which to chasten her mother or keep it as a bargaining chip later when she wanted something? Maybe she would just give it to her father and let him handle it any way he saw fit.

For months, she had wished her father would stand up to her mother's bullshit and file for divorce. She was a daddy's girl, after all. It hurt her to see him being used. Her father was a good man. Everyone who met Dennis liked him. Of course, Constance more than liked him. He was more of a nurturer than her mother ever thought of being. Her father did not deserve what her mom dished out. Even if they had to live in relative poverty, Constance vowed that if he ever decided he had had enough and left her, she would go, as well. She would stay with him no matter what, even if that meant changing schools.

Lauren saw Constance palm the condom wrapper and became

instantly furious, as much with herself as with Constance. It was a gross miscalculation on her part and damage control was going to be extremely delicate. Hell, it was going to be next to impossible. Making eye contact, they shared an angry, knowing look. In that tense moment, without saying so much as a single word, the two of them locked horns: sharing a fierce connection only a mother and daughter could. Lauren's look conveyed, *You don't want to mess with me, little missy.* Constance's eyes returned a defiant *Bring it!*

Trying to break the tension, Bradley looked up. "Miss Hill, I thank you. I think we're in agreement, from here. I think we'll just wait for the verdict." Then, glancing at Dennis and even sizing him up a bit, he continued. "And let me just say, you do have a very lovely family." And then he was gone.

Rose stood still waiting for further instruction. Before Lauren could issue any, Constance burst out, "Dad?"

"Yes, sweetheart?"

"Can I talk to Mom—in private?"

"I guess, if it's okay with your mother."

"Whatever, it's fine," Lauren interrupted, brushing him off with a second flip of the hand.

Rose and Dennis shared an uncomfortable look. Rose, not wanting to get involved in an obvious family squabble, kept silent. Dennis nodded, and the two wisely vacated the room. Lauren closed the door behind them.

Mother turned to daughter, tapping her foot in sheer displeasure and the two glared hard, not so much at as into one another. Their eyes focused into four, intense beams. It was an intense standoff. As much as she never wanted to admit it, Constance was becoming a great deal like her venomous mother. Lauren was proud of her intuitive offspring, although, in her eyes, she had a long way to go. It could very well be a hard lesson, but Lauren was going to show her just who the boss still was.

Constance Hill, in a calculated wordless display, coolly crumpled the opened and noticeably empty condom wrapper between her delicate fingers. The distinct sound of crinkling cellophane filled the room.

As the seconds waned, it became painfully evident the reaction she was hoping for was never going to materialize. She was sure that having the irrefutable evidence of her mother's infidelity in the palm of her hand would have scared her into an unavoidable and sincere apology. That, unfortunately for her, was not the case. The only thing she had accomplished was pissing her mother off. Her fatal assumption was that her mother still cared enough about her marriage to want to save it.

At that point, Lauren couldn't care less. She was tired of everything, especially having to keep up with appearances. Secretly, she was glad the charade was over. She produced an equally defiant I-could-give-a-shit smile and waited. After a moment, the annoying crinkling ceased, and Lauren walked to the wastebasket next to her desk in long, confident strides and picked it up. Holding it at arm's length to her daughter, she said nothing but waited for an appropriate response, the only acceptable one.

Her mother still had the upper hand. Mom paid for everything: the house, cars, clothes. Constance went limp in defeat. She complied. Taking her arm from behind her back, she reached up and dropped the damaging wrapper into the trash. Lauren looked at her as if to say, *Good girl,* removed the plastic bag, and tied it tight. Then she walked to the door and opened it.

Rose was packing her things to leave and talking to Dennis when Lauren opened the door and spoke her name. Both she and Dennis were startled.

"Yes, Ms. Hill?" Rose asked, rushing toward her.

Lauren waited until Rose was by her side, then whispered explicit instructions to her secretary to discretely dispense of the half-empty plastic bag she was holding in front of her between her thumb and forefinger. It was as if she were handling something dirty or even toxic. In an awkward transfer, Rose took the bag in like fashion, holding it at arm's length.

As she was about to shut the door, Lauren saw a disturbing sight. God walked through Rose, past Dennis, and, looking directly at her, headed straight toward her office. She marveled at the fact neither of them so much as flinched. Lauren slammed the door and jumped back. Undeterred by this feeble attempt to keep Him out, God effortlessly glided through the wooden fibers, stopping to survey the room before silently taking His place on the sofa.

Exasperated with her mother's stall tactics, Constance started tapping her foot. She was beginning to think she had made a colossal mistake giving up the discovered evidence without so much as a fight. Heck, without so much as a whimper. "Well, aren't you going to say something?" she demanded.

Lauren, recovering, turned to face her daughter. "Like what?" Lauren said, watching Constance's every move. *God,* she thought, *she even has my movements down pat.*

"I know." God's voice resonated inside her mind. He hadn't spoken aloud, but Lauren had heard it just as clearly as if He had. Startled for the second time in as many minutes, she jolted her head back. God looked unfazed, a gleam in His eye. He gave her that I-call-it-like-I-see-it nod. Lauren felt as if she were being tag-teamed.

"Aren't you at least glad I came to see you?" Constance impatiently asked her mother.

Still looking at God, Lauren replied, "Unannounced?"

"I texted you."

"Well, I didn't get it," Lauren answered.

"Well, I did. Maybe you were already . . . busy."

Not taking the bait in front of God, Lauren responded curtly, "I would have been home shortly, anyway."

Constance had needed to see her, wanted to see her, if only to catch her in the act of infidelity. What she discovered was about as close to confirmation of suspicions as one could get without actually walking in on them having sex.

"You could have seen me then."

The way her mother had coated her words with sarcasm brought Constance to the verge of tearing up. Instead of comforting her daughter, Lauren rolled her eyes, and this did not go unnoticed by God. He sat patiently, saying nothing. Lauren saw the expression on His face and toned it down, but only somewhat.

"Well, you're seeing me now. What is it?"

Constance was poking around her mother's desk, mustering up the courage to respond. Then, seeing the printout of Scripture, Constance picked it up and, changing subjects, asked, "You were reading this?"

Lauren quickly snatched it away. "It's private."

"They're Bible verses."

"I'm well aware. What do you want, Constance?"

Constance wasn't quite sure what she wanted, actually. She wanted a mother who gave a damn, that was for sure, and possibly a good wife for her honorable father. He deserved so much better. Then it came to her. She looked toward the sofa. The words came, rolling effortlessly off her tongue.

"I want you to change."

"Change how?" Lauren threw her hands up in the air, exasperated. First the Almighty and now her daughter: everyone was demanding something of her.

Constance shuffled her feet, pausing nervously and gazing once again across the room. Finally, "You cheat on Daddy," she blurted.

"That's none of your business!" Lauren scolded, resisting a glance toward God.

"You're not very much of a mother!" Constance exclaimed,

tears welling.

"Don't you dare tell me that!" Lauren blurted, beside herself. "What do you want me to do, stay home and bake cookies all day?"

"I want you to care!"

"About what?"

"About me. About Daddy!"

Lauren could resist no longer. She felt compelled by a not-so-gentle tug, an unexplainable force pulling her to look at Him. When she did, God was sitting there, stoic, offering nothing, but staring sternly. That only made Lauren angrier. She wanted to speak her mind, to lash out at Him. However, in front of Constance, she felt she had to convey sanity and make a good show. Nothing and no one was going to take the upper hand from her.

"Okay, so how do you want me to care about you? Exactly how?"

Intimidated, Constance didn't know how to respond.

"Well, when you figure it out, let me know. That would be great. In the meantime—" Lauren trailed off.

At that moment, something rather disturbing caught Lauren's eye. Constance was looking at the sofa, and from her expression, it was clear her daughter was seeing something or someone. *Could it be?*

"I don't know what to say," Constance said. Only the words weren't directed toward her mother, but the couch.

Her heart in her throat, Lauren asked, "Who are you talking to?"

Shuffling nervously, Constance said nothing.

"Answer me, Constance."

Meekly, Constance replied, "God."

"God? *God?* What do you mean?"

"God, Mom!"

"Where? Where is He?"

"Sitting right there." Constance pointed.

God smiled in acknowledgment when Lauren turned.

"What?"

Lauren felt a surge of emotions. On the one hand, she was angry at God for playing games. He most certainly could have revealed Himself to others at any time but had chosen to make her believe she had bought a one-way ticket on the crazy train. On the other hand, she was also ecstatic to know it was all real and not conjured up inside a diseased mind. She was hurt, frightened, and euphoric all at the same time.

I'm not crazy, she thought. *I'm not!*

"Aren't you God?" Constance asked.

"I Am."

"You see Him? You honestly see God, with your own eyes?"

Lauren rushed over to God, and placing a gentle hand on His face, she began to stroke His cheek. Like a sculptor molding a featureless lump of clay into a bona fide masterpiece, Lauren pulled and kneaded the Lord's face.

As patient as He ever was, God gazed up at her with the most adoring expression.

"That's God, Mom."

"Just stop," she said, closing her eyes. "Wait. You are seeing God? Truly seeing God?"

"Mom, you were just touching Him. Are you okay?"

Lauren was completely blown away.

"You both can see me. I've allowed it."

"Okay, stop. Just everybody stop." Then, turning to Constance, Lauren said, "How long . . . how long have you—" she trailed off.

"How long have I been talking to God?"

Lauren nodded.

Constance cocked her head and thought about it for a minute. "I don't actually know."

"Now, Constance," God began, gently scolding her for the white lie.

"Okay, since I prayed to Him," she admitted.

"You prayed to God, and just like that, He showed up out of the clear blue." Then, turning to God, furious, "She prayed to you, she PRAYED to you, and you—"

"What is there to marvel? At one time, you used to pray to me, as well."

"Yeah," she fumed, "a lot of good that did me. You never showed up in a fancy, three-piece suit to answer any one of my prayers. But you answered hers! Unbelievable! What does she have to pray about?" she pointed to her daughter. Turning to Constance, she said, "Seriously, what do you have to pray about?"

Lauren was beside herself with nearly thirty years of pent-up hurt and frustration. She had no idea what to do with her emotions or how best to let them out. It was all too surreal to be real. Yet Constance was there, flesh and blood, and unless the girl was just as crazy as she herself felt, it all had to be real.

Lauren looked over at her desk. The intercom was lit up.

"Yes, Rose?"

"Ms. Hill, Mr. Thompson is on the line. Says it's urgent."

"All right, put him through."

A short, crackly silence was followed by Rose telling Ryan that Lauren was on the line.

"Lauren, Maze is on his way back to your office!" Ryan blurted.

"Great, that's all I need." One more act added to the circus already taking place within the big top that was her office. "Why?"

Ryan sighed on the other end. "I was trying to talk to him about what you said and—" Ryan's voice trailed off.

Lauren turned to see God and Constance sharing a pained stare. She could see her girl was on the verge of crying. God reached up with the gentlest of touch and dried her eyes. He didn't wipe them away, but merely brushed her cheek and they instantly disappeared as if they were never there in the first place.

Uncharacteristically, Lauren's exterior began to melt away.

Seeing the truly emotional scene play out before her eyes and feeling the immense pressure, she cut Ryan off. " Ryan, listen! I have to go. I'll deal with Maze."

Lauren rolled her eyes. She didn't know exactly how long she had before Maze would burst through the door, but she didn't want her family present when he did. She had more than enough going on without psycho-boy ruining things.

CHAPTER TWENTY-FOUR

L auren composed herself and rejoined God and Constance. Even though the Lord had valiantly attempted to comfort Constance, she could sense her daughter was still not doing well. Inside, Lauren melted. The moment called for compassion. It called for action. But would Constance accept a kind gesture coming from her at that point?

Still, she had to try. Slowly, she walked to her daughter's side and knelt. Then, looking up, blocking God out of her immediate vision, Lauren gazed into her eyes and for the first time noticed how lovely a woman Constance was becoming.

She has my eyes, she thought.

Gently, she took Constance by the hand. Her voice was soft and reassuring. "So . . . tell me, then, what did you ask of God?"

To Lauren's astonishment, Constance was receptive. "I just prayed," Constance replied, nervously.

"I understand. But what, specifically, did you pray for? Can you tell me? Do you want to tell me?"

Constance and Lauren turned to God. Although He said nothing, the look God gave in return was nonjudgmental and kind.

He never seemed to change, never condemned. Through every encounter she had had with The Almighty, God had remained the same even-tempered, encouraging Creator of the Universe. Unlike earlier times, this demeanor now put Lauren at ease.

Pleased with Lauren and the progression of the conversation as of late, God nodded for Constance to continue.

"I prayed," she said, lowering her head, "and I asked Him to make me not dead to you."

"You're not dead to me, sweetie. What's that mean?"

Coming out of her shell, Constance poured her heart out. "Everything, everything comes before me!"

Still feeling a desire to defend herself, the natural self-preservation mechanism everyone has, the basic need to save face, Lauren explained the enormous pressures of work and responsibilities on her shoulders. Trying, at first, to justify her actions, Lauren caught herself in mid-sentence. It was her turn to lower her head in shame.

"I'm sorry if it seems things come before you and that I've made you feel less than loved."

"You never get around to me. Never, ever!" Constance sobbed.

Lauren wiped away her daughter's tears, trying to figure out how to spin it so it didn't put her in such a bad light. She was grasping, still desperately needing to come out on top. However, everything she could think of would only make matters worse. Before Lauren could say something she would only regret later, God intervened.

"Mother."

That one word, "mother," stated in tender inflections, surprised Lauren. She turned in awe of Him. He was truly a marvel to behold, and she hardly had enough restraint not to jump up and caress the Lord God. Finally, getting the response He deserved, God rose from the sofa in amusement. Suddenly, before Him on the coffee table were Buckyballs, those small magnetic balls.

Instantly, they broke apart and rose off the table. Effortlessly, they floated and circled Him, playfully. As He controlled their every synchronized movement, The Lord began to speak.

"Ah, the lesson. 6:16. Yes, that very 6:16. Do either of you know why they are called the Seven Deadly Sins?" he said.

Still marveling at the floating Buckyballs, the two humans shook their heads *no*. The Lord chuckled and waved at Constance's hair. With swift, tiny motions, the girl's hair began first to twitch, then to rise. Long strands lifted, intertwined, and braided. Her hair was styling itself: going from straight to shimmering waves and curls in fractions of seconds. Both women stood in awe. Sculpting and crafting, God continued.

"Now, Dillon, Dillon who was Saul, was certainly the clearest and closest when he said that to openly practice these vices one 'shall not inherit the kingdom of God.' He spoke truth. However, My Kingdom is neither a unit of good nor a component of privilege. It is not something to inherit. My Kingdom is freely given and active to those who believe, like a child born unto parents; the child does not inherit the air in order to breathe. And air is given without measure."

Without the slightest motion, God allowed the Buckyballs to drop to the floor. As He crossed the vacant space of the room, seemingly on their own and acting in unison, they began to converge, to consolidate, making geometric shapes, animals, and other configurations pleasing to the eye.

"My Kingdom, which can also be yours, just as the Earth is yours without having created a granule of it; My Kingdom, so we say, is always present. It is as present as either time or space. More so, for without Me or My Kingdom, there is no time or space. But you wonder and tax yourself, what of this kingdom and its opposite? Fear not, you are always in My realm. I have not taken My hands from you. You are always within My Kingdom. Do not be alarmed at what you feel you must do. Move further in any particular direction, by any means, of any modality. You are always in My Kingdom."

He paused to look lovingly upon them, then continued. "The kingdom can be understood as a two-story home. The first floor, where you congregate, is the domain of the mind. Up the stairs to the second floor, in the private quarters, is the realm of the heart. The home, itself, is your person. The rooms on each floor, the creations of your creativity and the levels, themselves, are the inspiration from whence you create. Though I am quite aware of monks, rabbis, popes, and even Dante allegorically using Proverbs 6:16, however, they are called the Seven Deadly Sins for a more practical purpose."

The two mortals stared, eyes wide with wonder.

God was pleased that they were listening to Him intently. He sighed. "For to engage in them forbids one from the pleasure of being alive. Surely, your body is able to perform the functions of a living, breathing soul—your mind can think, your heart can surely feel—but that, in and of itself, does not in absolute, define life. To be alive is to be present in the moment. For each moment is the only moment there is, was, and ever will be, that is, until the next moment, which may or may not come. That isn't promised to you. Yes, this is all wordy and sounds philosophical, but be not confused in the slightest. I am not a philosopher. I am the Truth expressed in all things. There is no time. There is no space. There is only that which is in the now. You can define it and measure it by a myriad of calculations, including time and space, but even they are dependent upon the existence of the 'now.' So, you see, there is only real and unreal, nothing betwixt and between. To be present is real life. Anything else is not real. It is like a blooming rose near one made of plastic of the same likeness or a person standing still next to their wax counterpart."

God allowed the Buckyballs to return to their original position upon the table. While the two women stood watching His every move, God made His way to the sofa and sat.

"Now," He continued, "back to 6:16. Isn't being locked in the moment with these seven vices real? Certainly not. It is the illusion of reality. To be present in the escape of being present is no satisfactory substitute for being present. What more proof do you need? What more difference need you? The difference is that between the heart beating, pumping its life-sustaining blood throughout the body, and one laid on a table, drained of its vital liquid and inanimate in its operation." A small smile of amusement played on God's lips. "Yes, they are both hearts, but only that which is real, animated, and functioning is important because that which is real is in fact living. To be absent from the present, that is, *real* life, is the equivalent of being dead, all the while tricking you with the appearance of being alive."

Lauren absorbed most of what God was trying to convey, but a few things confounded her. Her daughter was simply resolved to listen.

"What do you want me to do? I can't be different than who I am," Lauren huffed.

"But you can make different choices so you can spend more time with Me."

Lauren ran out of excuses. Throwing up her hands, she turned to God. "Okay, okay, I surrender. What should I do? What is it I should do?"

God sat stoically in a non-answer to her question. She knew exactly what was expected of her. It was left up to her to decide whether or not she was going to conform to it. Choice, it always came down to choice. There was nothing left to add or, for that matter, subtract from His precious word. Yet Lauren's face still expressed a clear yearning for a direct answer to a simple but vital question. God smiled. He wasn't going to let her off the hook that easy. His smile broadened and watched Lauren practically crawl out of her skin with anxiety.

He answers my daughter's questions. Why not mine? she thought. Again, she threw her hands up and turned to Constance. Just then, in the stillness of the room, a divine gust of wind brought a sheet of paper off her desk to her feet. Lauren looked at God. He stood and smiled kindly. Lauren stooped to pick it up. It was the printout of 6:16 Rose had given to her earlier.

"Is this it? I'm a sinner? I have sinned in Your eyes?" she said, looking down at the printout. "Is this what I am supposed to do, confess my sins? Confess that I am a sinner?"

"No," God said with a chuckle. "Ask, and your sins will be forgiven. You were never condemned in the first place, except to the extent that you suffered from your own agonized guilt. I never condemned you for any transgressions, although, certainly, it was Me you transgressed upon."

Although she was unsure of what to do or exactly what was expected of her, Lauren looked at Constance and blurted, "Well, I do. I confess. I confess to all these sins. Every one of them. Lust. Greed. Pride. Envy. It doesn't stop, and I don't even know where to begin to reverse it."

"Mom!" Constance ran and embraced her mother. Lauren embraced her back, as she had caressed her when she was just an infant, a time long forgotten.

"I'm so sorry, baby girl. I do love you."

"I love you, too, Mom."

"I am your mother and always will be. I love you."

Together, they shared a long, overdue cry. God stood, pleased with the outcome.

"My sins," Lauren started. "They are forgiven? They are? That's all?"

"Go and sin no more. As I commanded it," God intoned.

"What if I sin again? I mean, these are character flaws. "

"You would do it all again? Seriously?" Constance interjected.

"No, not like that. I didn't mean it like that." Her tears dried.

"Wait! Wait! So, you prayed to God, and He just showed up. And, and God revealed himself to me because of you? Because you think I act as though you were dead to me. Do I have it right?" Then, turning to God, "Let me ask you this. This girl, who has never set foot in Sunday school, doesn't attend church and isn't subjected to the word of God, mentors, ministers, or nuns, and Yet she prayed to you." Turning back to Constance. "How many times, my dear, did you pray to God this prayer?"

"I don't know. Never before, never like that."

"And so," she said, turning back to God, "You answer her. In all Your majesty, power, and wisdom, and pomp and flesh and blood, You answered her! And her wish was for a mother who is more motherly." Exasperated with God, she sighed. "Well, why, I ask You, why didn't You answer another little girl's prayers, a girl whose mother went crazy and tried to drown her or show her visions of what wasn't there! I remember that little girl who went faithfully to church and Sunday school every week."

The longer she talked, the more incensed Lauren became. "Where were You then? How come You didn't show up at her house, in the bathroom, or maybe in the barn, something in the least bit miraculous to show her You were listening? What is so damned special about this girl? I'm sure there are hundreds of children crying out to You hungry and homeless at this very moment!"

God stood and slowly walked to the picturesque window. "You demand an answer? You want to know why? Let me see. As a lawyer, wouldn't you say you're assuming facts not in evidence?"

"And, what facts are those?"

"Where I was, what I did, how your prayers were indeed answered."

"Present your evidence," Lauren stated, smugly.

God shot her a scolding look. "I need not, nor will I defend myself to you in a way pleasing to your ignorance and self-sown madness. However, I will cite a difference between the prayers you remember and the prayer of this sweet child of mine and temporary child of yours. All prayers and sounds are mere show if they do not originate from the heart. Anger, fear, and prayers to solve self-inflicted problems are vastly different. It's one thing to love and another to need. The heart loves, yet the mind, ah, the mind, it is incapable of loving. The best it can achieve is to think it desperately needs. And it calls that love."

Lauren was not impressed.

"I am not deaf, to be sure, but I only have an ear for the voice of the heart just as you would hear a barking dog over other distractions. Yet that does not mean I do not respond or reply. Maybe you never wanted things to be the way they were, but wasn't your mother sent away and your fear resolved?"

"Yeah, but not my heart."

God extended his arm toward Constance. "Behold, the embodiment of your heart."

A glimmer of light. Finally, true love dawned on her like the rays of the morning sun. Lauren gazed at her daughter with that newfound love. But the moment of quiet awakening was shattered when . . .

The intercom buzzed.

"Ms. Hill!" a distraught Rose chimed. "Mr. Maze is—"

Suddenly, the doors to her office burst open, and Lauren's world was once again thrust into chaos.

CHAPTER TWENTY-FIVE

"*I loved my wife!*" Maze screamed as he burst into the room. One second Lauren and Constance were sharing a very special mother-daughter moment. Blubbering and distraught, Maze managed to stagger inside, followed close behind by an equally distraught Ryan Thompson. Maze was in obvious pain and bleeding from the side of his head. Lauren scanned him, trying to assess the problem.

Maze was having obvious difficulty remaining upright. He swayed back and forth just inside the doorway, panting and gripping the left side of his face. He looked like he had barely escaped a war zone. Between his trembling, stubby fingers, copious amounts of blood oozed from a gaping hole in the man's head. Large drops fell from his now blood-soaked shirt onto the beige carpeting.

At first, Lauren couldn't process what could have happened to Maze. Constance stood gasping in horror. Lauren looked around for His Divine Holiness, but God had vanished. Just when they needed Him most, God had chosen to vacate. "Great, He's gone! Now what?"

Then Lauren saw something in her client's right hand. Maze was holding the disfigured, fleshy portion of what looked like an ear—his ear! "Oh, gawd!" Lauren exclaimed, turning Constance away from the horrific scene. The girl, however, had recovered from the initial shock nicely and was trying to maneuver around for a better look.

"Don't!" she said with curiosity. Constance gently pushed her mother away. "I wanna see."

Lauren looked at her as if to say, *You're a sick individual, my daughter.*

From the other room, Dennis, along with an extremely pale and obviously nauseated paralegal secretary, rushed through the opening.

"Someone get towels," Ryan said.

"I'll call 911," Rose exclaimed. She knew she should have gone home when she had the chance earlier. She darted toward the door, more to avert her eyes from the ghastly scene than in the performance of any real civic duty. She was not used to seeing blood, and this was not a simple finger prick. It was as bad a wound as she had ever seen.

"No!" Lauren instinctively yelled to her. "Wait!"

"We have to get him to a hospital, Lauren!" Ryan cautioned.

"Lauren!" Dennis shouted. "Ryan's right!" In his eyes, there was only one option. His wife's client had possibly life-threatening injuries. He was in danger of losing too much blood. That would be one ethical breach, not to mention a major lawsuit. He and his wife could lose everything.

Lauren put a hand to her forehead, attempting to block outside distractions and concentrate. She didn't have time to lose. Quickly, she weighed whether to take him to the hospital. If Maze went to the hospital, they might be able to save his ear, but there would be questions, a lot of questions about his mental state. On the other hand, if they could somehow bandage him up there, Maze would certainly lose the ear, but he wouldn't jeopardize his freedom.

The secretary's phone rang.

Another distraction. "Rose, your phone is ringing!" Then, under her breath, Lauren continued her thought. *And please, please let it not be that the jury's reached a final verdict.*

Rose didn't have to be told twice. She rushed out of the room to her desk.

Turning to Maze, Lauren scowled. "WHAT THE HELL HAVE YOU DONE?" she screamed. She had never been more outraged at a client's behavior. Maze could see how upset she was, but he was dealing with far too much on his own to be scolded.

"I couldn't take it anymore! I loved her!—I loved my wife! Aaaghh, it stings!"

"Well, what the hell did you expect?" Lauren said.

Just then, Rose reappeared at the entrance, bringing Lauren's worst fears with her. "The jury's ready." She looked up at the clock. "You have to be there in an hour."

Lauren's obsession with time made her look up to the clock. 9:33. She buried her head in her hands. "Damn. Ryan?!"

"Yeah."

"Quickly, see what the hell we have in the medicine cabinet. Gauze bandages . . . anything. There must be something to stop the bleeding."

"You can't be serious, Lauren!"

"Just do it!" she demanded.

A minute later, Ryan returned with a few packets of sterile bandages, gauze cling wrap, and a roll of medical tape. Ryan quickly rushed Maze to the restroom, followed by a disheveled Lauren pushing an uncooperative swivel chair on wheels.

Dennis followed her. "Lauren—"

"Not now! Wait in my office."

Like a well-trained puppy, Dennis obeyed.

Lauren set Maze harshly down in the chair while Ryan tore open the bandages with his teeth. "I'm a lawyer, not a paramedic, Lauren."

"Just do the best you can!" Lauren threw her hands up, pacing back and forth. She kept looking down at her watch, watching the seconds tick away. She was worried, beyond worried. She was frantically obsessing over how she could possibly get her client cleaned up and ready for court in less than fifty minutes. All that blood! Hell, she didn't even have courtroom-suitable attire for him. *This is impossible. Couldn't they have convened in the morning?* she thought.

"Take your hand away and hold this to your head." Ryan demonstrated to Maze. To him, it looked grotesque, worse than anything he had ever seen. The evidence was still in Maze's hand. The deformed, nearly colorless piece of flesh dangled between his fingers. This was way out of Ryan's league. Maze needed professional medical attention, and he needed it quickly. No way was the ear going to make it until after the verdict was rendered, even if packed in ice. If it wasn't sewn on soon, the tissue would die, and Maze would be permanently without it. And then what?

"Where the hell is your head, Lauren?" Ryan muttered.

Fresh blood oozed down the side of Maze's face as Ryan harshly applied the sterile bandages. Maze reached up to press them to his head as Ryan hurriedly wrapped.

"You cut your ear off; you cut your fucking ear off! I don't understand this," Lauren huffed.

Calmly, Maze looked up at her, puppy-eyed. "I loved my wife," he said, matter-of-fact.

"What the fuck does that have to do with pulling a Van Gogh and CUTTING YOUR FUCKING EAR OFF?"

Maze's eyes were clear, focused. After a long pause, with straightforward articulation, he calmly stated, "Because I DID kill her."

Silence! All movement ceased.

Lauren looked at Ryan, mouth agape. Their mutual suspicions were confirmed. Lauren had known there was something about that last conversation she had with him, something not right about him. Immediately, the two lawyers were thrust into a new situation. What the hell were they going to do now?

They had to leave and get their client cleaned up to face his verdict. They would deal with their ethical dilemma later.

"Rose, call the janitorial service. Let's get this mess cleaned up."

A crew was there within the hour, cleaning the drying blood from the walls and carpeting. No one spoke aloud; they only whispered amongst themselves, speculating what act of violence had taken place for there to be so many spatters. Except for the missing yellow police tape, it looked like a murder had taken place. The tenant was going to have some serious explaining to do. It was going to take some time and a great deal of scrubbing to lift the drying stains.

Dennis was sitting on the sofa in practically the same position God had been earlier when talking to Constance. For Constance's part, she seemed distant, distracted. She kept looking around as if searching for someone. There was something different about her, as well, a sophistication which he could not place a finger on. Her movements were no longer those of an awkward teenager, but those of a graceful, young woman. But there was something more. Then it hit him. With all the commotion, he hadn't noticed.

"What happened to your hair?" he said in amazement. "Did your mother do that?"

Of course she had. She had to have. Only the two of them had been in Lauren's office before all hell broke loose. It was just that it was so stunningly beautiful. There hadn't seemed to be hardly enough time for Lauren to pull off something so intricate. Constance swiveled her head, gracefully careening to look around. No, he had never seen Lauren, or anyone else for that matter, perform such braid work. Dennis looked down at his watch. He could not for the life of him figure out how Lauren could have styled their daughter's hair so professionally in such a short span of time, without so much as a comb. He looked around. No dyes. No cream rinse. No curlers, pins, or brushes. Why should there be? It was a lawyer's office, not a salon. Yet the weave was flawless, as if his lovely daughter were going to a ball. Constance was radiant.

"No," she said, flatly. She continued to stare into space.

Dennis was flummoxed. It wasn't like her to lie, and there didn't seem to be enough time for it to be done, but her hair was undoubtedly coiffed. It hadn't been like that fifteen minutes ago. *Okay, I get it,* he thought. Constance was making jest, poking fun at him because it was all too obvious. All kids do that.

"Are you looking for your mother?"

"No."

In actuality, Dennis had been growing tired of sharing a house with two of the opposite sex. Lauren was a loaded cannon, and Constance was becoming too much like her for his taste. Two Lauren Hills under one roof? Uh-uh. No way. He would go insane. Lauren was a lost cause, but his beloved daughter? Exasperated with her flippant, one-word answers, Dennis rephrased. "Then who are you looking for?"

God was nowhere to be found. Giving up the search, Constance approached her father. "No one. Nervous, that's all."

"Oh, I see," Dennis said, lowering his head. "I'll just have to file this one under teenage, 'I've got a secret.'"

"No, Dad." A constrained laugh. Constance sat down next to her father and placed a hand on his. Something was indeed on her mind. "Dad?"

"Yes," he said, putting his arm around her.

"I was wondering," she began. "How come we never go to church?"

Surprised by not only the randomness but also the general

uncomfortableness of the subject matter, Dennis sat back, eyes widening. He turned from his daughter, hand resting under his chin in seemingly deep contemplation.

Dennis was at a loss for a true, meaningful explanation. Initially, plenty of excuses came to mind, but as he gave them careful consideration, he found all his answers seemed lame at best. Sure, Dennis sometimes wrote late into the wee hours of the morning, especially on weekends, but that was only because Lauren did not want to have close contact or be bothered by him. He had long since given up trying to getting close to her. He merely busied himself to save face.

Dennis thought about giving Constance the standard, almost cliché excuse that busy lives simply got in the way of meaningful worship. Only that was the farthest from the truth. Alone, Dennis would sometimes halfheartedly pray to a God who didn't seem to listen—at least not to him. He would start and then drift off, thinking himself unworthy to address a sovereign God. Lauren made him feel worthless, not only as a husband but as a man. He didn't deserve a Savior. What was the point of getting up early on a Sunday morning to attend a service when his wife couldn't be bothered going with him to church or anywhere else?

Dennis might have written several unpublished novels, but he wasn't good at lying. Besides, he knew his intuitive daughter was much smarter than that. Constance would be able to see right through any lie or misrepresentation. Anyway, she deserved the truth. As much as it could sometimes be inconvenient, the truth was always the best way. It saved having to cover up the initial lie with even more lies at some later point in time.

Yes, the truth was he could have adjusted his writing schedule to different, more appropriate times of the day. He was alone in the household much of the day. And besides, it was not as if he were a bestselling author.

After a moment of awkward silence and coming up empty as to

why he had never made an effort to take his family, he felt guilty.

"If I had early on, maybe things would have turned out differently." Finally, he turned to his daughter. "I don't know, actually. We just never have. Why?"

Constance rubbed her father's hand. "I think maybe it's a good time to start."

He couldn't have agreed more.

CHAPTER TWENTY-SIX

Maze, Lauren, and Ryan were still in the restroom. Client and counsel exchanged hard glances. Of all the times Maze could have chosen to pull a crazy stunt, this had to be the worst. Flat out, Lauren did not feel sorry for him. If Maze was going to walk through the remainder of his life with a gaping hole in his head, so be it. That was his own stupidity. Since she was in charge, there would be no hospital visit. *Hope he never needs glasses,* she scoffed inwardly.

Ryan was dutifully applying medical tape to the gauze wrapping around Maze's head to hold his hurried work in place. All in all, it wasn't that bad of a job. At least it was fully covered.

Maze still held the dying tissue of his ear in his hand, a macabre souvenir he couldn't seem to part with. He flipped it up and down, nervously playing with it. Of course, Ryan still adamantly believed they needed to get Maze to a hospital, but Lauren was not budging. He turned to her. She seemed a million miles away, deep in thought. The latest developments had certainly caused distress; however, this was a time for action.

For the first time in her career, Lauren was in the unenviable position of needing to be in two places at once. After what had happened in court the previous two days, she wasn't about to postpone the verdict. What would she tell Her Honor, that her client was in surgery getting his ear reattached after self-mutilation? That would go over like a loud fart in a crowded elevator. Bandages could be explained away: a fall, a nasty cut. No one was going to unwrap it and check until after the verdict was given. Something had to be sacrificed. She decided that sacrificial lamb was going to be Maze.

A dark, rather noticeable red spot was growing on the side of Maze's head. Not good. Needing to be in court in—thank you very much, Lady Rolex—exactly forty-two minutes didn't grant Lauren nearly enough time to collect her thoughts. What she wouldn't have given for the jury not to have reached a verdict until morning or, better yet, that God would intervene and slow time to a crawl and allow her to recalculate the best course of action? Yeah, that'd be great. Silence greeted her question. Still, Lauren knew without a doubt He had heard her plea. She felt it. Only God, in His infinite wisdom, chose to watch from a distance. *He wants to make me squirm,* she thought. In the deafening quiet, she assumed she had her answer. She was seemingly on her own.

"There we go," Ryan said, standing back to admire his finished masterpiece. "Not too bad," he tried to convince himself.

"Okay, okay. We have to talk." Lauren started. "Wait. Never mind. Just stay put," she gestured with her hands to Maze. "Stay right where you are while Ryan and I figure out a game plan."

Maze winced but nodded.

Lauren gestured for Ryan to come with her with an abrupt nod of the head, and the two of them briskly headed out. As they made their way to the exit, God entered. He did not open the door but simply walked through it. Ryan saw nothing and continued walking. She stopped and turned, about to address the Lord as He brushed by her, but He never made eye contact. Without even the slightest acknowledgment of her presence, He continued on. In fact, she had to take evasive action, or He would have walked through her, as well.

Ryan turned toward Lauren and, seeing her concerned expression, asked if she were okay.

"Yeah, what could possibly be wrong?" she answered sarcastically. Lauren turned behind her to see a flash of intense, white light. "C'mon, let's go."

Ryan held the door open to Lauren's office and waited for his employer to enter. Constance stood, and Lauren rushed in to hug her. It pleased Dennis to see the exchange of affection between the two women in his family, even if only temporary. The tension between mother and daughter, as of late, had been more than he could bear. For him, this was a momentous occasion. It meant there was still a glimmer of hope.

Glancing at her watch, Lauren got right to the point.

"Listen, sweetie, Ryan and I need to strategize our next move. If you would like to see the verdict—"

"Awesome!" Constance was beaming.

"Wonderful!" Lauren beamed back. "Then you and Dad need to go down to the courtroom. I'll see you there, shortly," Lauren said, looking down at Dennis.

"Okay, Mom!"

Dennis stood, preparing to leave. Gloom came over him, although he produced a forced smile. Lauren hadn't even spoken to him. Instead, she quickly kissed her daughter, ushered her family out, and hastily closed the door behind her. At least she had mended her relationship with their daughter. That was at least some consolation.

As soon as he heard the latch click into place, Ryan spoke. "What the hell are we gonna do?"

"The bandage?"

Ryan gave her that don't-play-games-with-me expression.

"The confession, Lauren! Didn't you hear what that idiot said, back there?"

Lauren went purposely to her desk. She may have looked collected on the outside, but inwardly she was a bundle of nerves wrapped tightly inside a constricting straitjacket. She hadn't smoked in weeks. In fact, she had thought she had kicked the habit. However, the present situation was more than she could handle alone. She needed help. She needed that nicotine calm. Fingers trembling, she fished around for the half-pack of Marlboro Lights she had casually tossed into the top drawer, along with one of those cheap Bic lighters. She recalled tucking it inside the foil wrapping. At least that's where she remembered putting them.

Lauren had briefly thought about throwing them away, but something had told her not to. She had thought there might come a day like the one she was having now, when she would need a smoke.

Her memory served her well. She pulled out a cigarette, clenched it between her lips, and almost lit the end. Filter end. Damn! She turned it around, shaking her head, and lit the tip. Smoke curled its way upward toward the ceiling as she took a long, calming drag. Lauren held it in her lungs, then blew out a large puff of smoke. Instantly, she felt the desired effect. Her hands ceased shaking, and she could think more rationally. Amazing how that worked.

Ryan watched her every move. Lauren looked at Ryan, blowing out a cloud of smoke. Finally—

"Nothing," she said, tossing the lighter back inside the drawer and shutting it. "We say nothing about Maze's admission. Attorney-client privilege. The prosecution needed to makes its case; we don't do that for them."

Flabbergasted, Ryan grabbed a large portion of his own, thick, black hair with both hands. They were in the presence of a murderer with just minutes to right a possibly wrong decision by a jury.

"That's it? Nothing? We say nothing," he fumed.

"Nope, we do nothing. Nothing at all. There's nothing to do. At this point, it would be unethical for us to betray Maze's right to an impartial trial by jury."

Lauren put the cigarette to her lips and drew inward. The tip glowed, yellow and hotter blue closer to where tobacco met flame. Ryan watched the smoke stream in disbelief. She exhaled a thick, gray cloud of smoke. She coughed.

"The best thing, the only thing we can do is remove ourselves. Besides, we don't know if Maze was confused, delirious, or what when he confessed. Given the circumstances, all that blood, he was likely not in the right frame of mind at the time." Lauren took another puff, feeling the tingling effect against her tongue. "Besides, it's far too late for that. The jury has already come to a verdict."

Seeing it all going horribly wrong, Ryan said, "Yeah, but what if it's the wrong one?"

"Everyday occurrence," she said, nonchalantly. "Happens all the time in this business."

"You're just thinking about the streak, your perfect record."

"No, I'm not!" Lauren snapped. She took another drag of her cigarette. She knew her words didn't come out forceful enough to sound convincing. Her expression and mannerisms also conveyed a different story.

"Yes. You are."

"If I am, it's only a little. But it's no longer in our hands to decide. They're legally tied. Understand, overall it's their verdict, their trial. Not ours." She took a final, nervous drag, exhaled, and crushed the cigarette on the edge of the desk. "In the scheme of things, we're just players in society's proceedings."

Just then, the doors flew open. Triumphantly, Maze entered the office, a long trail of gauze and crimson bandages fluttering behind him. Ryan leaped to his feet in complete shock. It wasn't what he saw, but what he didn't see. No blood. No gaping hole.

No severed tissue. Nothing! Maze was once again whole. His ear was intact, and exactly in the location it should have been. No hint of evidence to suggest Maze had ever butchered it.

Pointing in disbelief, Ryan managed, "Oh, my gawd!"

"Don't say that!" Lauren snapped. Then, more subdued, she went on. "Not here. Not like that."

Staring intently at the impossibility of Maze's restored ear, Ryan stuttered. "Why?"

"Don't take the Lord's name in vain in this office."

"Huh?" he thought, snapping out of it. Now, he wasn't so sure the figure standing before him was in fact Maze, at all. He glanced at Lauren, then quickly back at Maze. "Since when did you get so religious?"

"In all seriousness," she replied, "about fifteen minutes ago."

Ryan barely heard Lauren's peculiar, under-her-breath reply. He knew something had been uttered, but it was lost on him. He was more concerned about Maze. He inched his way closer and closer to him, half out of fear, half curiosity. Initially, fear was winning, but the more he believed the person standing in front of him was indeed the same man he left covered in bandages in the office restroom, the more curious he became. A forensic scientist he was not, but he was compelled to get a closer examination.

"How in the . . . no blood . . . no sutures. Hell, there isn't a hint of scarring! Even the stains on your clothes." Ryan tugged on Maze's jacket. "Explain this!"

Maze thought Lauren knew who he had encountered in the other room, but he did not think Ryan would do well knowing the truth. Maze looked to Lauren for help. He didn't know exactly how to explain his miraculous introduction to God. He simply looked at Ryan, curious and puzzled.

Ryan reached up to take hold of Maze's earlobe and tugged at it. "I can't believe this. It's impossible! I don't understand," he trailed off.

"C'mon. We don't have time for this." Lauren broke in. "We have to go."

"Go?! Lauren, look at this!"

"I see it."

"It's a miracle." Then, turning to Maze, she said, "How did you—?"

Inside Maze, tension was building. Having his own worries, he looked as if he were about to rupture. "Am I guilty, now?" Maze blurted.

"What do you mean?" Lauren asked, delighted the subject had finally changed.

"I just confessed."

"Right," she began, glancing at Ryan before continuing. "Well, not necessarily. No, no, you're not guilty, yet. And the jury may not have found you guilty."

Maze's anxiety was kicking in full force, and having no medicine to counteract the oncoming panic attack, he was losing confidence as well as hope. His breathing grew heavier, and he began to sweat. Lauren could see his face turning red before her eyes. "But I am guilty. You have to tell them I'm guilty, don't you see? Isn't that what you have to do, now tell them what you know?"

"No. Pull yourself together. You don't confess to me. I'm neither your priest nor pastor. I'm not your conscience. I am your counsel."

"Is it too late for me to confess?" Maze said excitably.

Morally, it was a tough question for Lauren. She purposely scanned the top of her desk. Spotting the printout of Proverbs 6:16, she picked it up. She knew exactly what the morally correct thing to do was. For the sake of justice, Amanda Maze, and possibly her own sanity, she needed to reveal the truth. If anything, Maze's in-laws deserved closure. Her family certainly deserved to know their loved one hadn't figuratively as well as literally gone off the deep end and plunged herself into oblivion. However, she knew there was a good possibility she had beaten Bradley. Finally honest, but only with herself, Lauren admitted she did not want to lose the case due to an eleventh hour and fifty-eighth minute, half-assed confession.

"What do you counsel, counselor?" Maze pressed.

Lauren's hand gently brushed against the words on the page. Her index finger glided across each of the Deadly Sins, one-by-one until coming to the word *pride*. Lauren focused on the bold, black letters. As she stared, the word seemed to burn across her retinas. Her finger involuntarily tapped the paper. She hoped she wouldn't regret it, but finally—

"It's up to your conscience."

Ryan was inwardly furious. Did he hear correctly? Did Lauren just leave it up to Maze to reveal the truth? Did she think her client was going to confess? *That's it!* he thought. *She isn't in her right mind.*

Lauren hadn't actually pressured Maze into keeping his mouth shut, but she might as well have. It wasn't what Ryan wanted to hear, but unless he was prepared to reveal what he knew and risk his career, which he wasn't, then it truly was out of his hands.

"If I don't confess—"

"Before the jury renders its verdict," Lauren interrupted.

"Yeah, before the verdict. You're saying I might walk?"

"Yes, you might walk."

Having had his own miraculous experience with the Almighty caused Maze to reevaluate his life and, more specifically, to dwell on what he had done. However, the thought of still being able to walk after confessing to two individuals, that is, as long as he sat quietly and kept his big mouth shut for once, appealed to him.

CHAPTER TWENTY-SEVEN

"Stick by me and say nothing," Lauren instructed Maze as they pulled up to the steps leading to the Los Angeles Courthouse.

Night had fallen upon the City of Angels more than two and a half hours earlier; however, it was as bright as if the sun had never set. The sidewalk and much of the steps were illuminated by high-powered lights from various news crews. Lacking only the red carpet, it seemed as if they were at the Oscars. Even though it was a few ticks away from eight thirty, the place was bustling with the usual suspects eagerly waiting for the jury's verdict.

Ryan slowed the car and maneuvered into the designated parking space. Before they came to a complete stop, swarms of reporters rushed the vehicle, thrusting microphones toward the passenger window and shouting a bevy of standard questions before the door even opened.

"How confident are you, Ms. Hill, that tonight's verdict will exonerate your client?"

"Mr. Maze, are you glad the trial is over? Do you have anything to say to the press, Mr. Maze, since you didn't take the stand on your own behalf?" The question struck a nerve, reverberating in his head, playing over and over as the camera bulbs flashed around him. Then came the question everyone wanted the answer to.

"Did you do it, Mr. Maze?"

Maze froze. Lauren, seeing her client in obvious distress and unable to deflect the constant badgering, took Maze by the hand and squeezed tight. Then, lowering her head like a raging bull, she stepped out of the vehicle and plowed her way up the steps through the throngs of salivating humanity. Dutifully, the reporters followed after, calling to Maze, trying desperately to get him to break.

Granted, Maze had been angry with his counsel on several occasions throughout the proceedings, one just recently, but at that moment, Maze was thankful Lauren Hill had taken command. He felt like a fattened pig in a slaughterhouse. Following his lawyer's lead, he too lowered his head and gratefully allowed himself to be tugged away from his would-be butchers.

Inside the courthouse, Lauren let go of Maze's hand and immediately sought her family. She spotted Constance and Dennis standing next to the drinking fountain. Altering her course, she made a beeline toward them, telling Maze to stay close. She wasn't about to let him out of her sight.

Constance immediately felt leery around Maze; after all, he was an accused murderer, and she had seen him not that long ago with blood pouring from his head. He gave her the creeps. She looked away, not allowing herself to make eye contact. Uncomfortably, she shuffled her feet.

"You'd better go in and grab a seat," Lauren suggested. "They go pretty fast, even at this time of day."

Bradley and his team were making their way down the long hallway toward the courtroom. Hearing the familiar sound of Lauren's high-heeled footsteps upon the marble floor behind him, Dillon instructed his colleagues to make their presence known without him and turned toward her. Patiently, he waited for

Lauren's family to vacate the area before suavely making his move. "Hello there, Counselor," he smiled.

Hearing Dillon's voice, Constance slowed to a crawl. Dennis followed her cue. Together, they watched Lauren from a short distance, but too far away to hear.

"Dillon, can I talk to you for a minute?"

"I was hoping you'd say that," he said, bristling with excitement.

"You two go in," she told Ryan. "I'll be right there."

Reluctantly, Maze and Ryan stepped inside the courtroom alone while Lauren took Bradley aside.

"I've decided not to drag it out. I'm filing for divorce tomorrow," Bradley blurted.

Lauren nodded, but only in understanding. Before Bradley could say another word, she jumped in. "I need to apologize to you."

"You? That's a first." Bradley snickered, then, "Seriously, what for?"

"Listen, we should never have done what we did."

"But I—"

"It was wrong," she said, focusing upon the seven deadly sins.

"Oh, back to the morality thing."

"Life matters. Love matters. And we can't have either of those if we distract ourselves with momentary pleasure to forget the pain. I can't tell you that you shouldn't get a divorce, but if you haven't confessed your mistakes and tried to love your wife more than before, then with all sincerity, I suggest you do that first, and then decide what is right for you. Okay?"

Bradley looked down at her in astonished disbelief. He had been expecting the conversation to go very differently. He had had it all figured out. He had been certain she was going to be happy with the news and be just as eager to pursue a life together. Now he realized that it was never going to materialize. He looked up, mouth agape.

"Now, come on, D.A., we have a verdict to be present for," Lauren said, and briskly walked away.

Bradley stood shamefaced. He had to have misheard her. Only those words, her gestures, and the way she turned abruptly away— it was *goodbye*. Had to be. No other explanation. Crushed wasn't the word for what had befallen him. His ruination was complete.

What the hell just happened? Dillon had never felt so low. He was at a loss for words, a loss for emotions. He was devastated. Nothing left to do, he slowly turned and walked dejectedly into the courtroom.

Lauren spotted Dennis and Constance still hanging near the outside of the main entrance. She approached her family. "I love you two."

"We love you too, Mom," Constance said, hugging her mother.

"Baby girl, do me a favor."

"Okay." Constance was ready.

"Go into the courtroom and find seats for you and your father. I have to talk to Dad for a minute."

Constance happily bolted toward the door. God had planted a bug in her ear. Things were going to be pleasantly different from that moment on. That brought a smile to her face. All children want the same basic thing: a family who loves them. Constance was no different. If her mother was willing to change, Constance was willing to forget about her infidelity.

Because of time constraints, Lauren turned to Dennis. Looking into his eyes, she got straight to the point. "Now, I haven't always been the best wife, or the best mother, for that matter."

"You can't say that. You've been under tremendous pressure."

"Let me finish, please, Dennis." Lauren stroked his lips, a gentle, hushing action. "I guess in my own way, I believed I was trying, but I ask you to forgive me for not seeing, for not trying harder and for doing things that were counterproductive." Lauren sighed. "I just want to say that I do love and appreciate you for who you are, all you've done, and continuing to love me through all my many faults. I'm sorry I haven't loved you the way I should, the way you deserved, but if you'll be patient," she winked, "I'll show it more. Then we'll see how long it takes before you've had enough of my love and affection."

"That sounds like a great problem to have," he said and gently kissed her. "I love you. Quick, you better get inside."

Lauren watched as the twelve members of the jury filed in and took their respective seats. As always, Lauren studied them, trying to read their facial expressions. Some were better than others at hiding how they had collectively decided. The burden seemed to weigh heavily on some, especially the younger members. That usually happened in these types of trials. A majority simply clasped their hands in front of them as if praying they had made the right decision. In the current case, Lauren couldn't tell which way the pendulum had swung. Controlled and dignified, the twelve sat in reserved silence. She was just relieved none of them had morphed into God.

Lauren glanced at Maze. Once again, he seemed nervous, but at least he was self-contained. He was sitting quietly, playing with his newly reattached ear. She didn't know it, but a peculiar tingling sensation was all that reminded him of his rash decision to disfigure himself. God had proved to be a gifted physician, the consummate healer. Noticing Lauren's stare, Maze produced a nauseatingly fake smile.

At the prosecution's table, Bradley was also trying to decipher the facial expressions of the jurors. Now, more than ever since his last conversation with Lauren, Dillon wanted the win—badly. He was an aggressive competitor. He couldn't stand to lose twice in one day, both his love interest as well as the case. Suddenly, the long-anticipated moment arrived.

"All rise," the bailiff announced. "Honorable Susan Howell presiding."

Judge Howell entered, in all her flowing majesty. She seemed a great deal more tired than usual. The hour was definitely late, but Lauren could tell there was something more to it, some underlying issue.

"Thank you. You may be seated."

Maze remained standing, pathetically biting his nails. If not for the gravity of the situation, it would have been comical. Judge Howell found nothing amusing and was about ready to voice her disdain when Ryan alertly pulled him down into his chair.

"Sit, Maze!"

"Would the foreman please stand."

"Mr. Foreman, has the jury reached a verdict in this case?"

"Yes, we have, Your Honor."

"Very well. Mr. Foreman, in the matter of the People vs. Martin Maze, case number LA 120-897 JP, as to count one, murder as defined by Penal Code 187, how you say?"

A deafening silence befell the courtroom as all eyes remained on the juror. "Not guilty."

Gasps of disbelief resonated through the room. Shouts of both joy and outrage echoed, depending on which side of the room one was sitting. Amanda's mother ruptured into heart-wrenching wails while her husband stood holding her in barely controlled anguish. Tears streamed down his face in shock as he pounded a clenched fist against his chair. Adding insult to injury, Maze's few supporters, as well as Lauren's family, cheered the decision. Anxious media in the press area bolted toward the exit, and suddenly, the courtroom was thrust into a state of semi-reserved chaos.

Over the sound of her banging gavel, Judge Howell's voice elevated.

"Order. Order."

"Your Honor." Bradley rose demanding to be heard. "I request to poll the jury."

Banging her gavel several more times, Judge Howell finally quieted the courtroom. "Very well, Mr. Bradley. You may proceed."

Bradley approached the jury and set his sights on Juror number one.

"Please inform the court. How do you find the defendant?"

Juror number One stared Bradley in the eye. "Not guilty."

"Juror number two?'

"Not guilty."

"Number three?"

"Not guilty."

A defeated Bradley turned slowly to his seat as the last juror confirmed what the jury foreman had already announced to the court.

"Thank you, Your Honor. I have nothing further."

Maze remained standing, in stunned silence.

Normally, Ryan would have been ecstatic, congratulating lead counsel on a magnificent performance. But for him, the sense of victory was subdued. Although they had won, justice had not been served. He sat, arms folded across his chest. Still, he managed to shake his head and produce a strained smile. His stomach churned.

Judge Howell sat poised, gavel in hand, raised above her head. The courtroom was quieting, except for the first row behind the prosecution's table. For the woman who had given birth to Amanda and the rest of her family, there was neither closure nor relief. If the man her daughter married didn't do it, and she had been struggling with the belief he had, then what had happened to her? Amanda couldn't have taken her own life. She just couldn't. On the day she had left on the cruise, she had seemed so happy. As much as her mother tried to regain composure, uncontrollable, involuntary sobs escaped her.

The gavel cracked. All motion ceased. Finally, Maze heard the words every defendant in a murder trial wants to hear and certainly the ones he had waited months to hear.

"Mr. Maze, you are free to go. This trial is adjourned. The jury is excused."

Maze looked up and smiled, realizing he had just been handed a new lease on life. It hadn't been granted to him, though. With the help of Lauren Hill, he had stolen it. Be that as it may, he would no longer have to think about the senseless murder, confessing his guilt, or spending the rest of his life behind bars. He embraced the acquittal and glorious freedom.

Maze looked across at the jury hastily filing out. One juror looked across at him, wondering if she had done the right thing. He winked and mouthed *Thank you* to her. Her heart sank. A nauseating feeling grew in the pit of her stomach. Saying nothing in reply, juror six quickly hurried ahead to join the others. Maze then glanced up at the bench to Judge Howell. A chill went up his spine.

Seeing the sudden change in her client, Lauren also looked toward the bench. God, dressed in pristine white robes in all His majestic glory, glowered down at Maze. Constance gasped from the back row, but not even her father heard her over the murmurings of the crowd.

God stood, displeased, throwing his robe to the side for effect. It billowed, fluttering to a controlled position behind Him. He only uttered one word, the contemptible name of the acquitted. "Maze."

CHAPTER TWENTY-EIGHT

Criminal psychologists and profilers alike have perused countless old photographs, chilling snapshots of seemingly innocent children turned ruthless criminals, hoping to gain insight as to what had taken place in their youth to foster such latent activity. Hours have been spent intently studying case files to learn the nature, the inner evils of the criminal mind. Traumatic experiences, molestation, neglect, and abuse have all played significant roles in the development of deviant behaviors later in life. While violence may be relatively easy to understand and pinpoint in some children, many other histories leave one shaking his head, wondering, "How could such an adorable, innocent child such as this, grow up to become a murderer? What happened between then and now?"

At the moment, Maze was asking himself those very questions, replaying parts of his own misguided childhood. Sure, his father had been strict, but never had he considered his discipline abusive. Okay, so his childhood home had been unconventional and harsh at times. Whose hadn't been? Every kid in the neighborhood had been beaten at some point. Yes, his father had been a weekend alcoholic, admittedly not the every-night-of-the-week raging drunkard many kids had to face, but from the first crack of a golden bottle of Corona after work on Friday until he staggered into bed late Sunday night, Carlos Maze had been a rip-roaring lunatic. He had been what Maze had called a "problem drinker." When he drank, Carlos had been a problem, to himself and others around him. He had been verbally abusive to anyone who crossed him, including his quiet-as-a-church-mouse wife.

To compensate for her husband's lack of affection and spousal abuse, she, in turn, had taken much of her frustrations out on her children, like most mothers in town had done. It had been the norm and Maze accepted it. It had been all he ever knew, how life had been supposed to be. He had learned at a young age to stay out late and avoid his entire block until his father passed out on the couch watching light porn sometime after midnight. Yet despite the seemingly unhealthy mentality in his home growing up, Maze believed he had turned out well. He hadn't joined any gangs, stayed away from drugs, and had a good paying job. His neighbors liked him; elders respected him. Maze truly felt as if he had arrived. That had been until the day he came home alone from his cruise. As soon as he had disembarked, rumors had started. How did everything go so horribly wrong? Maze didn't have an answer. Tears welled.

The gavel pounded, bringing him back to reality.

"Stop!" Maze yelled.

Heated comments and conversations ceased. Maze looked around the room, stopping momentarily at the key players in his recent life: Lauren, Ryan, Amanda's parents, Bradley, Judge Howell, and, coming down from the bench, God Himself.

Visibly shaken, Maze blurted, *"I did do it! I did kill her! I killed my wife!"*

Shock and awe! Everyone in the room except Ryan and Lauren was stunned. The silence was maddening. Wanting to act, the bailiff turned and looked to Judge Howell for direction. Only the jury had already been dismissed. What could she do? The rule against double jeopardy now came into play. Maze was a free man.

Judge Howell was beside herself. She realized that law was not an exact science. Not every criminal who came before her was convicted and sent to prison. Several, she had even released on minor technicalities. But the law was the law. As flawed as the system sometimes was, it was the way it worked. If law enforcement hadn't conducted themselves and performed their job professionally or had obtained evidence illegally, a judge had no choice but to let the accused go free. But this? This was the first time anyone had confessed just moments after being found innocent. As she searched through papers, Maze continued.

"I threw her overboard," Maze bellowed. "We had a fight. She was suicidal." The more he talked, the faster he spoke. "She accused me of not loving her, not caring about her. She was manic! I loved my wife, but I killed her. Without the grace of God," he said, looking directly at God, "I killed her."

God wasn't slowing but walked briskly toward him. Maze felt trapped, his eyes shifting back and forth. The bailiff placed his hand on the holster of his revolver. If Maze were to act, it had to be now.

Impulsively, Maze sprang into action. The weight of guilt and shame combined into too much of a burden to handle. He felt compelled to confess his crime in front of both God and man, but he couldn't bear to face the consequences that went along with it. All he wanted to do was to end his miserable existence and join his wife in the great beyond. But he had to act immediately.

Lunging at the barrier separating the spectators from the trial, Maze thrust his entire weight upon it. Wood splintered with a loud snap.

One of the columns broke off into a nearly perfect, jagged stake. Ryan dove for it, but Maze seized it first. With as much force as he could muster, Maze swung at the young attorney, slashing a considerable gash across Ryan's right forearm. Blood immediately seeped through Ryan's shirt as he tumbled backward, landing awkwardly on his back. Lauren rushed to his side and applied pressure, positioning herself between the junior attorney and her crazed client like a lioness protecting her cub in an unselfish act of motherly protection.

Judge Howell, never having witnessed anything of that nature in her courtroom, stood ineffectively gaping as the scene unfolded before her. Her indecisiveness frustrated the bailiff. No longer waiting for the judge to recover, he took charge.

"Freeze!" he said, drawing his weapon. In all his years as a bailiff, he had never had to unholster it. Its mere presence had always been enough of a deterrent.

Out of options, Maze had to act fast. Placing the stake on the hardwood floor and prepared to thrust himself upon it. Just then—

"*Maze.*"

Maze turned to the calm, soothing voice of God.

"Don't move, mister!" The bailiff shouted, cocking back his pistol.

"Maze, this is not the way."

"But I killed her," he wept.

Thinking Maze was addressing him, the bailiff got down into a low stance. "Put it down, now!"

"Your sins are forgiven you, My son."

"But I killed her," Maze sobbed, looking up at God through blurred vision.

"This is the last time I'm gonna say it. Put it down," the bailiff ordered.

"Still, they are forgiven," God reached out a hand to him.

The bailiff applied pressure to the trigger. He couldn't allow things to escalate any further. *If this guy insists on playing games, I'm ending this,* he thought.

"You forgive me?" Maze said, dropping the stake. Slowly, he stood, placing his hands obediently in the air.

"Yeah, buddy, I forgive you," the bailiff said, lowering his pistol. "Get your hands behind your back." Then he added an afterthought as he cuffed him: "You have no idea how close you came to meeting God, just now," Two uniformed officers rushed in to assist.

"I never condemned you, Maze," God reassured him. "Now, come with me."

Turning to the bailiff, Maze smiled. "Already have."

"Takes all kinds. Come on, walk."

The three officers led Maze out of the courtroom. It wasn't the added presence of the two officers flanking each side keeping him in check, but the firm, gentle grip of the Father upon his left shoulder.

Dennis and Constance, seeing it was safe to move, ran to Ryan and Lauren. With their combined help, Ryan was able to get to his feet.

"Just a scratch," Ryan winced. "I'll be okay. War wound." He smiled. Then, turning to Lauren, "I didn't think you cared."

"I don't," Lauren smiled.

The gavel banged. "Can we please have a medic in here," Judge Howell shouted from the bench. She was glad things were beginning to quiet, but she honestly couldn't wait to get back to her chambers. She needed a drink, the stiffer, the better.

Dennis ripped Ryan's shirtsleeve open. "Good, it's not arterial. You're gonna be okay."

"What the heck made him go off like that? One minute he was fine, the next—" Ryan trailed off in contemplation.

"His conscience. Couldn't live with himself anymore: his crime or the lies to cover it," Lauren suggested.

Constance lovingly hugged her mother, glad she had not been injured in the melée. "Mom, are you going to represent him again if he asks?"

Lauren looked up at the great seal of California, glad to put the trial behind her. But she was certain she was going to be okay. More than ever, she was looking forward to that long-needed vacation, but this time, she'd be on that beach with her husband and daughter beside her. Lauren sighed and glanced down at her daughter.

"Not *no*. Hell, no."

9 781633 936522